Slipping deeper into sleep, into her waiting dreams, Rainey sighed as images of Buck pulled at her, teased her, stirred fantasies she wouldn't allow to surface in the light of day.

With a murmur that was his name, she turned into her pillow, reaching for him, aching.

The phone rang suddenly, like a scream in the night. Startled, Rainey jerked awake, her heart thundering like a runaway train. "What...?!"

Confused, she thought her alarm was going off, only to realize it was the phone. Blindly, she reached for it in the dark. "'Lo?"

"Stay away from Buck Wyatt," a cold male voice growled in her ear. "If you help him find the mine, you'll live to regret it."

Dear Reader,

I'm so excited about *Fortune Hunter's Hero,* the first in my new series, BROKEN ARROW RANCH. In the past, when I've written connecting books, each book was still relatively independent of the others. In this series, the mystery continues throughout all four books. Putting the concept together was a real challenge—I loved it! The first story is about Buck Wyatt, who, along with his three sisters, inherits a ranch in Colorado, then has to live there for a year in order to meet the terms of the inheritance. During his stay at the ranch, he meets Rainey Brewster, a fortune hunter who travels the world in search of lost treasure. Together, they share a series of adventures that lead to the kind of love neither thought they would ever find.

Writing the story was great fun. I hope you enjoy reading it as much as I loved writing it.

Linda Turner

Linda Turner

FORTUNE
HUNTER'S HERO

Romantic
SUSPENSE

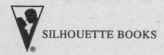

SILHOUETTE BOOKS

ISBN-13: 978-0-373-27543-4
ISBN-10:   0-373-27543-9

FORTUNE HUNTER'S HERO

Visit Silhouette Books at www.eHarlequin.com

Printed in U.S.A.

Books by Linda Turner

LINDA TURNER

began reading romances in high school and began writing them one night when she had nothing else to read. She's been writing ever since. Single and living in Texas, she travels every chance she gets, scouting locales for her books.

With special thanks:

First, I need to thank my mother, Margie Turner, for believing in me even when I refused to be on the school newspaper in high school.

My agent, Lettie Lee, and my editor, Gail Chasan, have always had great faith in me, especially over the last few years, when my life turned into a roller coaster. Thank you both so much for your continued support and patience.

And last, but not least, I'd like to thank Frank Bays for keeping me on track—and on deadline—throughout the writing of this book. Thank you, honey, for that...and for keeping your head in the middle of a hurricane in Mexico. What would I do without you?

Prologue

London, England

Seated with his three sisters in front of Clarence Jones's desk, Buck Wyatt lifted a dark brow at the solicitor who had worked for the family for as long as he could remember. "All right, we're all here, as you requested. What the devil's going on? What's the big mystery you couldn't talk about over the telephone? Have we won the lottery or what?"

A slight smile curling the corners of his mouth, Clarence only shrugged. "Possibly. It all depends on you."

"Are you having a scavenger hunt like you had for your birthday?" Priscilla asked him, intrigued. "You wouldn't tell us anything then, either."

"Oh, I hope so!" Katherine said, delighted. "What's the prize this time? How about a week in Monte Carlo? That would be marvelous! I'll invite Peter—"

"No one said anything about a scavenger hunt or the lottery," Elizabeth pointed out dryly. Studying the older man with narrowed eyes that missed little, she warned, "Watch it, Clarence. You're beginning to resemble kitty when she swallowed the canary. Cough up your secret before we have to pound it out of you."

"There's no reason to get physical, Lizzie." He chuckled, his green eyes twinkling behind the lenses of his glasses. "I do have some good news...possibly."

"What do you mean...*possibly?*" Buck retorted. "It either is or it isn't good, old man. Which is it?"

Far from offended—he'd been a family friend long before he'd become the Wyatts' solicitor—Clarence chuckled. "Patience, my dear boy. All in good time." Sobering, he opened the single file that lay in front of him on his desk and added, "I received a copy of Hilda's will yesterday from her attorney."

Whatever Buck had been expecting, it wasn't that. He'd only learned of Hilda Wyatt's existence three months ago, when he received a letter from her informing him that they were cousins—her grandfather and his great-grandfather were brothers. The two sides of the family had lost touch decades ago when Buck's great-grandfather moved to London in 1902 as a diplomat, and there was nothing Hilda wanted more than to get the family back together.

Surprised, Buck was in total agreement. He was named after his great-grandfather, who had been quite an adventurer, and one of Buck's most prized possessions was his namesake's journals. Reading them as a young boy, he'd been fascinated with the stories his great-grandfather had written about growing up on the family ranch in Colorado. When he was nine, Buck had promised himself that one day he would go to the States and see the Broken Arrow Ranch—if it still existed—firsthand.

Hilda not only confirmed that it still existed, but she'd invited him and the girls to visit next summer. Thrilled, Buck had just begun making travel arrangements last month when he learned that Hilda had unexpectedly died when she'd fallen and broken a hip.

Buck had only spoken to her a few times—he barely knew her—but her death had still come as a shock. Besides his sisters, she had been his only living Wyatt relative, and he'd been looking forward to getting to know her better. He'd had hundreds of questions about his American ancestors, and now those questions would never be answered.

"Why did her attorney send you a copy of her will?" he asked with a frown. "We'd only spoken a few times. I seriously doubt that she would have left us anything. She didn't even know of our existence until three months ago."

"That may be," Clarence agreed, "but she was a spinster and had no children. Leaving the ranch to family was important to her—which is why she left the ranch to the four of you."

Buck couldn't have been more stunned if he'd told him the queen had left Buckingham Palace to him and his sisters. "You can't be serious!"

The solicitor smiled slightly. "It's in the will, if you'd like to read it."

"We have a ranch?" Priscilla exclaimed, a look of pure horror on her face. "With cows?"

"You don't have to say it like that," Elizabeth chided. "You make it sound like Hilda left us a bunch of rattlesnakes or something." Struck by the thought, she turned to Clarence with wide blue eyes. "Oh my goodness. I suppose there are snakes on a ranch, aren't there?"

"In all likelihood," he agreed, amused. "Though they won't be a problem in the winter."

"Winter—summer…a snake's a snake," Katherine retorted, wrinkling her nose in distaste. "I don't want anything to do with them."

"I still don't understand why she left the ranch to us," Buck told Clarence with a frown. "She lived there her entire life. Even if she didn't have children, she must have had a lifelong friend she could have left the place to."

"The ranch has been in the family since the 1850s," he replied. "Apparently, she didn't want to be remembered as the one who gave away the ranch."

"So she left it to total strangers?"

"No. She left it to family. With stipulations," he added.

Priscilla sat back with a sigh of disgust. "Here it comes. The strings. Why are there always strings?"

"Hear the man out," Katherine told her. "It may not be that bad. Maybe she just wants us to make sure there are fresh flowers on her grave every month."

"Actually, Hilda's stipulations are a little more involved than that," Clarence said dryly. "One of you has to be at the ranch at all times for a period of one year."

"You mean we can't leave?" Elizabeth asked, surprised. "For an entire year?"

"Oh, any given three of you can leave at anytime," he assured her. "You can come and go, changes places, trade out—whatever you want to do. But for the period of one year, one of you can't be absent from the ranch for two or more consecutive nights."

"And if we are?" Buck asked. "Things come up. We could agree to the stipulation then find ourselves going in four different directions when life interferes. There's no way to predict what's going to happen over the course of a year, Clarence. You know that. What happens if one of the girls gets seriously sick and ends up in the hospital? You know we'll all be there. What happens then?"

"The ranch goes to an unnamed heir," he said simply.

"For one infraction?" Katherine asked sharply.

He nodded grimly. "Hilda left a sealed letter, naming a new heir, with the will. I have instructions to open it only if you choose not to accept the terms of the will or you can't fulfill Hilda's stipulations. If you *are* able to complete the year without a problem, the letter will be shredded and the ranch is yours."

Glancing from Buck to each of his sisters, the older man lifted a grizzled brow. "Well? What do you think? Is this an impossible task for the four of you or do you think you can pull it off?"

"Pull it off?" Priscilla exclaimed. "How can we? I don't know about everyone else, but I don't want to live in the wilds of Colorado! There can't be any decent clubs there. And they drink ice in their tea, for heaven's sake. How barbaric is that?"

Elizabeth grinned. "They also drive on the wrong side of the road!"

"Oh, God, you're right," Katherine groaned. "We'll have to buy an American car and learn to drive all over again. We'll have to take a driving test, won't we? On the wrong side of the road!"

"Don't blame the roads." Buck laughed. "You'd have a hard time passing the test here at home again."

"Just because I like speed—"

"Don't fight, children," Clarence said dryly. "That's not why you're here."

"He's right," Buck agreed. "You're all worrying about nothing. You can stay here. I'll go to America."

"Forever?"

Buck had to laugh at Priscilla's horrified tone. "I'm not going to the moon, Pris, just Colorado. You know I've always wanted to see the ranch. This is my chance."

"What about Melissa? Don't you think you should discuss this with her first?"

At the mention of his fiancée, he smiled. "Melissa

was all set to go with us to the ranch before Hilda died. I don't think she'll have a problem with the move. She's been wanting to visit the States for a long time."

The girls exchanged a speaking look, but none of them pointed out that visiting a country and moving there to live were two different things. Instead, Clarence arched a thick gray brow and said, "Then you agree to accept the terms of the will?"

Buck looked at his sisters. "Well?"

Priscilla hesitated, but in the end, she nodded, along with her sisters. "If you need a break and need someone to come and stay for a while, we can take turns flying over."

The matter settled, Buck said, "When do we have to be there?"

"By Friday."

"*Friday!*"

When they all spoke in unison, he grinned. "I'm just following the instructions in Hilda's will." Reaching into the top drawer of his desk, he pulled out a set of keys and handed them to Buck. "Joshua Douglas, Hilda's lawyer in Colorado, forwarded these to me, along with the copy of her will. If you have any problems when you arrive in Colorado, he will be happy to help you."

"As long as we're not absent from the ranch for more than two consecutive nights," Elizabeth pointed out. "Then he's going to evict us and hand the place over to someone else."

"I have every confidence that between the four of you, you're not going to let that happen."

"No, we're not," Buck said grimly. "My grandfather told me stories *his* father and grandfather told him about growing up on the ranch. And they all left written records of their life on the Broken Arrow. We're not going to be the generation that loses it."

Chapter 1

Broken Arrow Ranch, Colorado
Four Months Later

"We've got another problem. The back-up generator's not working."

In the process of replacing a dripping faucet in the kitchen, Buck looked up at his foreman with a quick frown. "You're joking, right?"

Even as he asked, he knew he wasn't. David Saenz wasn't the kind of man who joked about much of anything. In fact, Buck had hired David four months ago, right after he'd arrived in Colorado and discovered the condition the ranch was in, and in all that time, he'd only seen David crack a smile a handful of times. Not, he admitted, that there was a lot to smile about. The family homestead that he'd been so anxious to claim as his and his sisters' inheritance was falling down around his ears.

Needless to say, he'd been appalled when he'd first seen the place. It was in drastic need of paint and repairs, not to mention a good old-fashioned cleaning, and he blamed the previous foreman for that. Hilda was eighty-four when she died and had obviously not been able to take care of the place for quite some time. Her foreman should have stepped forward and made sure, if nothing else, that basic maintenance was done on the house, barns and equipment. Instead, the man had, apparently, collected his paycheck and done little else except take advantage of a little old lady who'd had no family to protect her. For no other reason than that, Buck had fired him.

When he'd put an ad in the paper for a foreman, David was the first man to answer. Buck would have hardly described his personality as sparkling and David had had no experience as a ranch foreman. He had, however, spent the last twenty years working as a handyman for a string of apartment complexes in Denver before he was laid off after being injured in a car wreck. He was healthy again and ready to work, and when he was able to easily fix a loose handrail on the stairs, Buck hired him on the spot.

Buck was the first to admit that working around the house wasn't his field of expertise. He was a stock-broker—or at least he had been until he quit to accept his inheritance. Over the course of the last four months, however, he'd come a long way when it came to working around the ranch. With David's guidance, he'd worked on the house and barn and vehicles and learned more than he wanted to about repairing leaky faucets and toilets and crumbling old fireplaces that needed new mortar. He didn't mind the work—in fact, he enjoyed it—but there was no time to appreciate the progress he and David had made. Something different seemed to break every other day, and the to-do list got longer and longer and longer. It was damn frustrating.

And they hadn't even begun to deal with the more serious problems that were threatening to tear the ranch in two. Fences were down, cattle were missing, and lately, he'd noticed signs of trespassers on the ranch. And he knew immediately what they were after. Gold.

Oh, he knew about the lost Spanish gold mine. Who didn't? Tales of the lost mine had been circulating in the area for well over two centuries, ever since the mine was lost in a landslide in the eighteenth century. Even his great-grandfather had written in his journals about how Spanish explorers had discovered an incredible vein of gold in the wilds of what was now the Broken Arrow Ranch, but they'd been forced to abandon it after an avalanche covered the mine's entrance and forever changed all landmarks in the area. According to legend, the massive amounts of gold the Spanish had taken from the mine were nothing compared to what was still buried deep in the mountains.

Not surprisingly, fortune hunters, adventurers and geologists had been looking for the mine for centuries, without success. Buck knew as long as the mine's location remained undiscovered, he would have to deal with trespassers who had no respect for what belonged to him and his sisters. For the moment, however, he had more immediate concerns.

Setting down the pipe wrench he'd been using on the kitchen faucet, he regarded David with a frown. "What seems to be the problem with the generator?"

"I think it's just given up the ghost. It's at least twenty years old. It should have been replaced years ago."

"How often is it used? Do we really even need it?"

"We're a long way from town, and it doesn't take much for the lines to go down. Ice in the winter, hailstorms in the spring and summer. And then there's brownouts. Whenever the electricity goes out, everything shuts down—the freezer and fridge, the air, the heat…"

It was that time of year, late spring, when the temperature could be in the nineties one day and it could be snowing the next. Last night, the temperature had dropped to seventeen degrees. Record highs were predicted for later in the week. Whatever the weather did, he planned to be prepared. "Then I guess we'd better replace it."

"I'll check around and see what kind of price I can get on one."

"What about the truck? How's it coming?"

The older man grimaced. "I'm charging the battery

right now. If that's not the problem, then it probably needs an alternator."

Buck didn't know if he wanted to laugh or curse. *If.* God, he was learning to hate that word. If the termites hadn't gotten to the studs in the bathroom wall, just the paneling would have to be replaced. If the sick cow that died that morning in the barn didn't have mad cow disease, the rest of the herd was probably going to be all right. If the well hadn't run dry, then the problem might be the pump.

And if the jackass Hilda hired as a foreman had done his damn job and not taken advantage of an old lady instead, Buck thought irritably, then he wouldn't be bankrupting himself now to put the place back on its feet!

Quit your whining, a voice drawled in his head. *It's not the ranch that's really bothering you, and you know it. It's Melissa.*

He couldn't deny it. What a fool he was, he thought bitterly. He'd believed that she loved him enough to follow him to the ends of the earth. Fat chance. She hadn't loved him—she'd loved a stockbroker who vacationed in Switzerland and Monaco and rubbed shoulders with the rich and powerful in London. She'd wanted nothing to do with the wannabe cowboy in the wilds of Colorado. She'd dropped him like a hot rock.

Forget her, he told himself coldly. She'd shown him who she really was, and he was better off without her. Besides, he had more important things to worry about—

like keeping the ranch that had been owned by his family since before the American Civil War.

He couldn't argue with that. In spite of all the problems he'd run headlong into, he didn't regret leaving London and moving to the ranch. He loved the place, loved the untamed wildness of the mountains and canyons, the isolation. Not for the first time, he wondered how his great-grandfather had ever found the strength to walk away.

Buck had only been here four short months and couldn't imagine living anywhere else…except when the pipes rattled and doors stuck and the roof leaked.

How many things could be wrong with one house? he wondered, a reluctant grin tugging at his mouth. After working on it from the moment he'd arrived at the beginning of January, he and David hadn't made a dent in anything except his bank account. If he was going to restore the ranch to its former glory—and he was determined to do so—he was going to need to win the lottery. Or find the lost gold mine…if it existed.

Grimacing at that word again—*if*—he sighed. "I'll check prices on a new generator and see what I can find. You might as well make a parts list for the truck, too."

"Good," David grunted. "Brake shoes need to be first on the list. They're just about shot. Oh, yeah, and fan belts. I don't think they've ever been changed."

"Make me a list," Buck said as he turned his attention back to the sink. "I should be finished here in about an hour."

Taking him at his word, David returned an hour later with a list that turned out to be pages long. Buck spent the rest of the afternoon tracking down parts and prices, and the final results weren't pretty. And it was only a partial list!

Sitting back in his chair at the massive antique desk that dominated the ranch office, staring at the outrageous sum he'd come up with, Buck found himself once again thinking of the lost gold mine. Maybe finding it really was the only solution. The ranch was turning into a money pit, and he'd hardly even tackled the ranching problems: downed fences, lost cattle, feed to get the animals through dry summers and long winters.

How the hell was he going to do this? he wondered, scowling. What little money Hilda had had at her death had gone for her funeral—the land was all she'd had to leave. He had his own money, of course, but the ranch wasn't his and his sisters' yet. Not for a year. He felt sure the four of them would be able to live up to the stipulations of Hilda's will, but he couldn't be absolutely certain of that. He'd already invested some of his own money in the place. How much more was he willing to risk?

Lost in thought, his eyes focused inward, he suddenly realized his gaze had fallen on the built-in bookshelves across from his desk that contained a number of books on the history of Colorado and life in the Old West. Several included references to the Broken Arrow and the lost Spanish mine—he knew because every time he got a spare moment, he read everything he could get his hands on about the ranch and its secrets.

Was the mine really out there somewhere, lost in the mountains? he wondered, frowning. Or was it just a rumor, a half truth that, over the centuries, developed into a fantastic story that was too good to be true? He didn't doubt that there probably was a mine that had been lost in an avalanche—there was too much historical evidence to dispute that—but how much gold had actually been taken from the mine? If it really was as rich as the rumors claimed, surely someone would have found it in the last two hundred years. He'd read reports from the geologists the Wyatts had brought in over the years—they were inconclusive. Was there any supporting evidence to back the rumors? Surely there had to be something....

Pushing to his feet, he strode over to the bookshelves that lined the entire east wall of the office, studying the titles of the books he hadn't yet read, and pulled out the oldest one. It wasn't until he dropped into his favorite easy chair to read that he realized that book was actually a journal written by Joshua Wyatt, his great-great-grand-father and the pioneer who first settled the ranch. Seconds later, he was totally lost in one of the most fascinating stories he'd ever read.

Rainey Brewster wasn't a woman who was prone to nerves. She'd been too many places, seen too many things. As a child, she'd traveled the world with her father, moving with the wind wherever whimsy and fate took them, searching for treasures that had been lost down through the ages. She'd slept in tents and castles, traveled by everything from car to plane to camel, and thanks to the teachings of her father, she recognized a two-legged snake when she saw one.

When her father died six months ago, she'd continued to run the business as he had, and though she missed him terribly, she couldn't imagine ever doing anything else. There was just something incredibly appealing about looking for buried treasure. Especially when she was hunting for one of those rare finds that the rest of the world had long since given up hope of finding.

The lost Spanish mine on the Broken Arrow Ranch was just that kind of treasure. And she was almost positive she knew where it was.

Approaching the front door of the Wyatt-family homestead, she smiled at that familiar tingling feeling she always got when she was closing in on a treasure. It seemed as if she'd been waiting for this day forever. During the last five years of her father's life, the two of them had, whenever they were in Spain, spent all their spare time researching the mine, checking state and private libraries all over the country, looking for any references to it, regardless of how small. It wasn't until three months after her father died that she stumbled across what the two of them had always dreamed of finding: irrefutable proof not only of the mine's existence, but of its location. Now all she had to do was convince the new owner of the Broken Arrow Ranch that she could make him rich beyond his wildest dreams.

Knocking sharply on the scarred wooden door that appeared to be original to the house, she assured herself that convincing Buck Wyatt to work with her was going to be a piece of cake. After all, he was British, educated, and according to the gossip she'd picked up in town, quickly running out of money. He'd already had a fortune in property fall in his lap. Surely he wouldn't turn his back on the gold mine sitting in the middle of it.

Determined to make him see reason, she squared her shoulders and once again lifted her hand to knock, but a split second later, the door was jerked open and suddenly, she forgot to breathe.

She'd done exhaustive research on not only the mine, but the Wyatt family, as well, and there was no question that the man who stood before her was a Wyatt. The Willow Bend library had worlds of data on the local ranchers, including pictures of the Wyatt family all the way back to the 1800s, and Buck had the same sharp eyes, the same rugged face and tall, rangy build as every Wyatt man who'd owned the ranch for the last hundred years. He might have been born and raised in England, but he had *rancher* written all over him.

"Do I have a fly on my nose?"

Jerked out of her musings, she blinked. "I beg your pardon?"

"As well you should," he retorted, amused. "You're staring at me like I have a bloody fly on my nose."

Mortified, she could do nothing to stop the hot color that bloomed in her cheeks. "I'm sorry. Really. I don't know what I was thinking." Abruptly sticking out her hand, she forced a smile. "You must be Buck Wyatt. I'm Rainey Brewster. I was wondering if we might talk."

He did not, as she'd expected, take her hand. Instead, he studied her with midnight-blue eyes full of suspicion. "Obviously, you didn't stumble up my driveway by mistake, and you're not part of the welcoming committee. They were here four months ago, and you weren't with them—I would have remembered. So why are you here, Ms. Brewster? What do you want?" His accent had turned clipped and very British, and for the life of her, Rainey didn't know what she had done to earn his suspicion. "I'm sorry," she said quickly, dropping her hand. "I should have called first, but what I have to say to you isn't something you discuss on the phone. If you have the time, I'd like to talk to you about the lost Spanish gold mine on your property."

"Really?" he retorted dryly. "And what business is that of yours?"

"I'd prefer not to discuss it on the doorstep…if you don't mind."

For all of ten seconds, Buck seriously considered shutting the door in her face. He didn't know who she was or what she wanted, but he had no intention of discussing the mine or anything else that belonged to him with a stranger…even if she was the cutest woman he'd met in a long time. If she thought she could use her looks and that sweet, dimpled smile to talk him around, she was in for a rude awakening. He wasn't so easily taken in.

"Actually, I do mind," he retorted. "I don't invite just anyone into my home. State your business, Ms. Brewster, and be quick about it. I'm busy."

He was being a hard-ass and wouldn't have blamed her if she'd called him a jerk and walked away. But the lady was tougher than that. When her chin shot up and her blue eyes glinted with irritation, he found himself impressed. She was a gutsy little thing.

"My business, Mr. Wyatt, is the mine. I'm a treasure hunter and would like the opportunity to discuss the mine's location with you."

Disappointed—God, another treasure hunter out to con him!—he groaned, "Not another one! Do you know how many people like you have knocked on my door over the last four months, Ms. Brewster? The family's been looking for the mine for well over a hundred years. My office is full of yearly reports from geologists and archaeologists and even Indian shamans who swear they know where it is, and there's no sign of gold anywhere. What could you possibly know about the mine's location that all of the experts missed?"

"More than you obviously think," she retorted. "The reason they haven't been able to locate the mine is because they're looking in the wrong place!"

Far from impressed, Buck laughed. "You know, for a moment, I actually thought you were serious. Nice try, love. Now that you've had your little joke, I suggest you leave. I've got work to do."

"Wait!" she cried when he started to shut the door in her face. "I'm serious!"

"Mmm, hmm," he said as he continued to shut the door. "You probably know where the Holy Grail is, too."

"Don't be an ass," she retorted. "I'm trying to help you! If you'd just listen—"

"To what? Another half-baked story about where the mine is? I've heard them all. Did you have a dream or what? One lady told me an angel appeared to her and told her. Then there was the drifter who claimed he heard it on the wind. Wow. So, tell me…why should I believe you? Oh, wait, I'll bet I know. You're psychic! You looked in your crystal ball, and there was the mine, right there in front of your eyes."

Heat burned her cheeks, but to her credit, she stood her ground. "You'll apologize to me in the future for that, Mr. Wyatt—"

"I don't think so, Ms. Brewster. But then again, I'm not psychic."

"Obviously not," she said, her blue eyes glinting with triumph, "or you would know that I'm not, either. I discovered the whereabouts of the mine in some private papers in Spain."

Far from impressed, he just looked at her. "Really? And you expect me to believe that even though people have been looking for the mine for centuries, you found papers that no one else even knew existed?"

Rainey couldn't blame him for his skepticism. Her claim *did* sound outrageous. "If you'll just take a look at what I have, you won't regret it," she assured him. "All I need is ten minutes."

For a moment, she thought she had him. He hesitated, studying her consideringly. Then his jaw tightened. "I don't know what you found in Spain, Ms. Brewster, or what you paid someone to create false documents, but you wasted your money. Now, if you'll excuse me, I have work to do—"

Lightning quick, she stuck her foot in the door. When he gave her an arch look, she merely held out her card. "When you change your mind, call me. I'll be in town for another week."

Making no effort to take her card, he just looked at her. "I have no intention of changing my mind."

Rainey rolled her eyes. God save her from stubborn men! "If people didn't change their minds, Mr. Wyatt, they would still believe the world was flat." Impulsively, she leaned forward and daringly tucked her card in his shirt pocket. In for a penny, in for a pound, she thought with a grin, and winked at him. "I'll be waiting for your call."

When he just looked down his aristocratic nose at her, she almost laughed. But her intention was to spark his interest, not irritate him, so she turned and walked away, feeling the touch of his eyes on her long after she drove away. He would call, she told herself confidently. He had to. Her father had spent years looking for the mine, and since his death, she had vowed to keep up the search in his honor. Now that she knew where the mine was, she couldn't let Buck Wyatt stop her. She would give him a week. If he didn't call, then she would show up on his doorstep again. Sooner or later, he was bound to give in.

Chapter 2

Rainey Brewster, Ph.D, historian, treasure hunter.

Scowling at the card she'd given him, Buck snorted. So now she was claiming to have a Ph.D. What kind of nutcase was she? Did she actually expect him to believe she'd tracked down some ancient papers in Spain and just that easily, discovered where the mine was? Yeah, right. And his great-aunt Matilda was on a first-name basis with the pope!

So just who was Rainey Brewster and what the bloody hell was she really after? Money? Why else would she have shown up on his doorstep? She claimed to have something he wanted—the location of the mine. Of course she expected him to pay for it.

If that was the case, she was nothing but a scam

artist, he thought, scowling, and he'd be crazy to trust her. For all he knew, she could be after much more than just money for telling him the location of the mine. She could be after the ranch itself. If she'd hooked up with the right person, someone who felt that he was the unnamed heir in Hilda's will, the two of them could have hatched some sort of plan to drive him away from the ranch before the year was up.

Buck tried to dismiss the idea as foolish, but he knew he couldn't be too cautious. The town was abuzz with talk of Hilda's unnamed heir. Was it her closest friend? A neighbor? A total stranger? The possibilities were endless, and so were his enemies, Buck thought grimly. Oh, no one had made any direct threats, or, for that matter, openly done anything to make him feel anything less than welcome, but he wasn't a fool. The entire community of Willow Bend, Colorado, thought Hilda was the last of the Wyatts and had, no doubt, expected her to leave the place to someone in the community. Instead, she'd willed the ranch to Brits she didn't even know, and that had to make anyone who thought they were the rightful heir bloody angry.

And who could blame them? The Broken Arrow was worth a fortune. How far would someone go to get the ranch back if they thought it rightfully should have gone to them? Considering the terms of the will, all they really had to do was keep him away from the ranch for forty-eight hours. How better to do that than to enlist the aid of a young, attractive fortune hunter who claimed she wanted to help him find the gold mine his family had been searching for for well over a century? How far would she go to keep him away from the ranch? Invite him somewhere and have car trouble? Lose her keys? Seduce him? Just what was Rainey Brewster capable of?

All too easily, he could see the spark of daring in her blue eyes when she'd leaned over and tucked her business card in his shirt. The lady was trouble with a capital T and he'd do well to steer clear of her.

Unfortunately, she wasn't the only one waiting for a chance to blindside him and keep him away from the ranch. All anyone needed was forty-eight hours. By the time the girls learned he was missing, they wouldn't even have a chance to fly in from London. Just that easily, the ranch would be lost.

Furious that he didn't have a clue which direction trouble would come from, he found it impossible to concentrate on the bills and paperwork Hilda had stuffed in boxes over the course of the last two years and just let go. He needed a break from the stress of trying to keep the place afloat, so he grabbed the keys to the Jeep, one of the two vehicles he and his sisters had inherited along with the ranch, and headed for the mountains in the distance.

Later, he couldn't have said how long he'd been driving when he noticed the temperature gauge on the Jeep had shot into the red zone. Swearing, he braked to a grinding halt and cut the engine. Before he could step to the front of the Jeep and lift the bonnet, a cloud of steam poured out from under the hood.

"Bloody hell!"

He wasn't a mechanic and what he'd learned about cars over the last four months wasn't nearly enough, but even he recognized coolant when it puddled on the ground beneath the engine. And even if there'd been a jug of the stuff in the vehicle—which there wasn't—it would have done little good. When he grabbed an old towel from the back of the Jeep and lifted the steaming-hot bonnet, he spotted the blown radiator hose instantly. Like it or not, the Jeep wasn't going anywhere.

"Well, you wanted to get away from everything, old chap," he told himself wryly. "Congratulations. You succeeded."

He had, in fact, more than succeeded. Glancing back the way he had come, he only then realized that not only had he left the lower grazing land of the ranch far behind, but he was already in the foothills of the mountains. Frowning at the far horizon, he bit back a curse when he saw nothing but undeveloped ranchland all the way to the horizon. The homestead was nowhere in sight.

Swearing, he reached for his cell phone, but one look at the out of range message on the screen had him swearing in frustration. So much for calling for help, he thought in disgust. And considering the fact that David didn't even know he was gone, the odds of the foreman coming to look for him were slim to none. There was no hope for it—he'd have to leave the Jeep and walk home. He'd be lucky if he got there by dark. Muttering curses, he started walking.

Two hours later, the sun was on its downward slide behind the mountains and his feet were killing him. Damning his footwear, he was seriously considering walking the rest of the way barefoot when he heard the sound of a vehicle in the distance. Five minutes later, David topped the rise in the beat-up old green pickup that was used for work around the ranch and caught sight of him in the distance.

"I've been looking all over the place for you," the older man told him. Glancing past Buck to the ranch road that disappeared into the foothills leading to the mountains, he frowned when he didn't see the Jeep anywhere. "When I couldn't find you at the house, I remembered the last time I couldn't find you, you were up in the mountains, checking out the elk. Where's the Jeep?"

"It died about eight kilometers back," Buck retorted, wincing as he stepped toward the pickup. "It blew a radiator hose. Why were you looking for me?"

"We've got trouble."

Buck shouldn't have been surprised. Every time he turned around, it seemed like something else was going wrong. "Don't tell me," he groaned. "The roof fell in."

"Well, not exactly," the older man replied, "but it could be just as costly. Someone cut the fence to the southern pasture and brought in a semi. From what I can determine, three hundred head of cattle are missing."

Buck took the news like a blow to the gut. "Son of a bitch!"

"The tracks are fresh," he added. "And since it rained last night and the tracks weren't filled with water, the bastards must have hit sometime today."

"In broad daylight," Buck said tersely, cursing.

He nodded. "The county road that runs by there doesn't get a lot of traffic. You can go by there just about anytime of day and not see a soul."

Buck wanted to believe that if someone had seen the rustling, they would have reported it, but he wasn't betting the ranch on it. People didn't want to get involved, especially if it meant siding with a foreigner over one of the locals. They'd just look the other way. And then there were those who were waiting for him to fail. They might even help the rustlers load their trucks!

"We've still got to report it," he told David grimly. "Let's go back to the house so I can call the sheriff, then we have to see about getting a radiator hose for the Jeep."

Not surprisingly, Sheriff Sherman Clark hadn't received any calls on the missing cattle and didn't expect to. "I'll check the cattle barns, but it's just going to be a waste of time. Anybody who rustles cattle these days isn't stupid enough to sell them right down the road. Those cows are probably halfway to Chicago by now."

"And you don't have any idea who might be responsible for this?"

"Oh, sure," he said easily. "I've got plenty of ideas, but ideas won't put anybody in jail. I've got no witnesses, no evidence, no cows, for that matter. And the tire tracks were brushed away. So all we know is that whoever did this didn't do it alone. They had help—a lot of help. Unfortunately, you can bet that whoever organized the theft made damn sure that his partners in crime were tight-lipped and knew how to keep their money in their pockets. Nobody's going to be wagging their tongues over this. There's too much at stake."

Buck didn't have to ask what he was talking about. The Broken Arrow was what was at stake. "So there's nothing you can do," he said flatly. "I just have to eat the loss."

"I wish I could give you better news," the older man said, "but unless you had the herd insured, you're looking at a total loss. And the odds are, Hilda didn't have insurance. She let a lot of things slide over the last couple of years."

"So I've discovered," he retorted. "Thanks for your help, Sheriff. I'll check into the insurance."

"Good enough," he said, shaking his hand. "If I hear anything, I'll let you know."

He wouldn't hear anything and they both knew it, but that wasn't the sheriff's fault. And it certainly wasn't Hilda's. She'd done everything she could to hold the place together, but she'd been old and alone and she'd left a will that, unfortunately, made him and his sisters the target of every jackass out there who thought he was the unnamed heir. And he had a feeling the situation was only going to get worse as the year deadline grew closer and closer. The question was…what the hell was he going to do about it?

The question nagged him the rest of the afternoon as he helped David repair the fence the rustlers had downed, then tow the Jeep back to the house and install a new radiator hose. And the situation only got worse when he discovered there was no insurance on the cattle. Then the new property-tax bill arrived in the mail. He took one look at it and started to swear.

Damnation, where did it end? Between the four of them, he and his sisters could come up with the money, but they didn't have an unending supply of money. And the ranch seemed to be a bottomless pit. If things didn't change—and damn soon—they wouldn't have to worry about losing the ranch because they were gone for forty-eight hours. They'd lose it to bankruptcy!

Disgusted, he needed a drink. All he had to do was step into the library and pour a Scotch and water, but he'd never liked drinking alone. Maybe he'd go into town, see what was going on at the Rusty Bucket. A local watering hole, it was the place to go to hear the latest gossip. Was there any talk about the cattle rustling? How many people knew about it?

The more, the better, he thought grimly as he headed upstairs to his room for a quick shower. The more people who knew a secret, the greater the odds that someone wouldn't be able to keep their mouth shut. All they had to do was confide in one person, and the news would be all over town. It was just a matter of time.

Forty-five minutes later, he stepped into the Rusty Bucket and wasn't surprised to find the place packed.

When he'd stopped by there his first week in town, nothing about the bar had impressed him. The tables were rough-hewn picnic tables, the lighting was dim to the point of nonexistent and everyone in the *joint*—he could think of no other way to describe it—seemed interested in drinking beer. There hadn't been a decent wine in the house. He'd almost left, then the waitress had recommended he try one of the steaks. He'd taken one bite and fallen in love. He'd been a regular ever since.

"Hey, Mr. Wyatt, it's been a while. Are you on the prowl for a little red meat?"

Greeting Rusty Jones, the owner of the bar, with a grin, Buck drawled, "There's nothing little on the menu short of a side of beef and you know it. I don't know how you stay so thin, Yank."

Tall and lean as a broom handle, Rusty chuckled. "It's in the genes, Your Lordship. We're a skinny lot. There's not a plump one in the family. Now…about that steak…"

"Actually, I just came in for a drink, but a steak's exactly what I need. I'll sit at the bar—"

The words were hardly out of his mouth and hanging in the air between them when he spied Rainey Brewster sitting alone at a table for two by the front window. She'd changed into a dark red sweater that did incredible things to her skin and eyes and she'd released her hair from the tight knot she'd had it twisted in earlier. Just that easily, she'd become soft and sexy and touchable. And she was looking right at him.

A smart man would have nodded a curt greeting and

headed for the bar. But he'd been thinking about her on and off all day, and suddenly, there she was, right there in front of him. What else was a man who believed in fate supposed to do?

"Never mind," he told Rusty, never taking his eyes from Rainey. "I'll join the lady at the table by the window. We have some things to talk about."

He never saw the surprise in Rusty's eyes, never saw the watchful stares that took note of his every step as he headed across the bar to where Rainey sat, seemingly waiting for him. How had she known to expect him? He hadn't known himself that he was coming to town until forty-five minutes ago.

Suspicion churning in his gut, he studied her with narrowed eyes as he reached her table. "Mind if I join you? Or are you expecting someone? I can sit at the bar—"

"No one at the bar can tell you where the mine is, Mr. Wyatt," she retorted simply. "Pull up a chair."

She wasn't smug, but there was a confidence in her blue eyes that told him that it didn't matter what kind of arrangement they finally agreed on, he was toast. She had something he wanted, and she knew it.

A smart man would have cut and run right then. But there was something about the way she challenged him that he found impossible to resist. So she thought she was clever, did she? Time would tell. Taking the chair across from her, he lifted a dark brow at her in amusement. "Who said I wanted to talk about the mine? Maybe I'm here for a steak."

"Maybe," she agreed easily. "So what are you saying? You're not interested in the mine? No problem. A lot of people think it never really existed, anyway. And maybe it didn't," she added with a shrug. "Maybe I misunderstood the papers I found in Spain. I'll be the first to admit that I'm not infallible. And the older the records, the more difficult they are to read and interpret. I could have misunderstood. My Spanish isn't perfect."

Flashing him a rueful smile, she reached for one of the menus and changed the subject. "So…what do you recommend? This is the first time I've been here. What's good?"

When she glanced up from her open menu, he just looked at her. "The truth," he retorted. "You don't believe for a second that you misinterpreted whatever you found in Spain. So why lie about it?"

Her eyes flashed at that. "I'm not lying. I'm just saying what you want to hear."

"You wouldn't still be in town if you thought you were wrong," he pointed out. "In fact, you seem like the type of woman who would be meticulous about research. You would have never approached me if you thought there was a possibility that you were wrong."

Surprised, she frowned, irritated. How could he know that? He didn't even know her. "What I know, Mr. Wyatt, is that, for whatever reason, you don't want to believe that the so-called *experts* have been wrong about the mine's location all these years. Why you would want to believe them instead of me since they haven't found the mine is beyond me, but that's your choice. I can't control what you believe."

The matter settled as far as she was concerned, she turned with an easy smile to the waitress as she arrived at their table to take their order. "I'll have the rib-eye and a baked potato with extra butter. Oh, and ranch dressing on my salad." When she turned back to Buck and found him watching her in amusement, she lifted a brow. "What? Is there a problem?"

"Not at all." He chuckled. "It's nice to meet a woman who's not always on a diet." Ordering porterhouse steak and a salad, he waited until the waitress had departed before focusing his attention once again on Rainey. "So tell me about your research in Spain."

She eyed him warily. "Why? So you can shoot me down again?"

His lips twitched. "Are you that easily discouraged?"

"If I was, I would have left town this morning," she said dryly. "I was hoping if I gave you some time, you would…"

"Come to my senses?"

"Something like that," she admitted with a grin. "And it worked! Didn't it?"

"Maybe." He shrugged. "Maybe not. This is your chance to speak your piece. Give it your best shot."

He didn't have to tell her twice. "I was in Spain, doing research in a university library on the lost mine, when I came across a reference to a family in Barcelona whose ancestors supposedly had come to America with the first Spanish missionaries. I traced the family tree, discovered there were descendants still living on the land the family had owned for three hundred years, and went to meet with them."

"And they told you everyone had been looking in the wrong place for centuries?" he said incredulously. "I find that hard to believe."

"I found proof in their library," she said quietly. "I have copies of excerpts from the diary of one of the missionaries. You're welcome to read them."

"So let's see them," he retorted as the waitress arrived with their food. Sitting back, he waited expectantly. "Well? I presume you have this evidence with you."

"I have it in a safe place," she assured him.

"This is a safe place. Let's see it."

"Yeah, right." She laughed. "Nice try, Mr. Wyatt. Do I, by any chance, have Stupid tattooed on my forehead?"

"I never said you were anything less than intelligent," he replied, amused. "Obviously, you're afraid I'll take your information and run with it, and in the process, cheat you."

She shrugged. "It's happened before, Mr. Wyatt—"

"Buck," he corrected her.

She hesitated, her eyes narrowing speculatively. "Our relationship is strictly business, Mr. Wyatt. There's no need for first names between us."

"Unless you detest formality, Rainey. I do. Now, about our deal—"

"We don't have a deal."

"Not yet, we don't. This is your chance, love. Go for it."

Rainey's heart stumbled at the casual endearment. It meant nothing, she told herself. He probably called every woman he knew *love*. So what did he call a woman he cared about? And why did she care?

Horrified at the direction of her thoughts, she jerked herself back to the situation at hand. After years of working with her father to find the lost mine, searching for clues all over the world, she finally had a shot at finding it. She couldn't blow this!

"I'm not just selling information," she told him. "I want to be actively involved in the search for the mine."

He lifted a brow at that. "You want to get those pretty hands of yours dirty?"

"Yes, I do," she said with a jut of her chin. "And I want a finder's fee and a percentage of the mine's gross for the first ten years of operation."

"Ah…money." He sighed, smiling slightly. "Why did I know we would get around to that? Just out of curiosity, how much is this supposed finder's fee you think you're entitled to?"

When she named a figure that by any stretch of the imagination was outrageous, he laughed. "Yeah, right. Would you like my right arm, while you're at it? Or maybe my firstborn child? I don't have one yet, but I haven't given up hope. How much time do you have?"

Heat climbing in her cheeks, Rainey gave serious thought to dumping her salad on top of his head. It would have been no more than he deserved. But even as her fingers itched to snatch up the bowl and send it flying his way, she reminded herself that she held all the cards. Why was she letting him push her buttons? She had a better idea of where the mine was than he did.

Sitting back, she surveyed him in amusement. "Is that a no?"

"What do you think? Of course it's a no!"

"Okay," she said easily, and took her first bite of steak. "Wow! This is incredible! How's yours?"

"Excellent," he said without tasting it.

"Really? I've never seen anyone taste something without taking a bite."

His lips twitched. "We all have our talents."

Rainey's eyes dropped to the sensuous curve of his mouth. He would be a good kisser, she thought, only to blink in confusion. Had she lost her mind? What was she thinking? The man stood between her and one of the biggest treasures she'd ever hunted. And all she could think about was his mouth? She didn't think so!

Thankful for the years of poker she'd played with her father, learning to bluff, she put on her game face and smiled. "You're absolutely right. I'm really good at finding lost treasure, but you're not interested in that. That's okay. I understand. You want to find it yourself. I can't blame you for that. I'll just move on to the next treasure. If you change your mind, give me a call. Maybe we can work something out."

He was a gambling man—she could see it in his

eyes—but he didn't, to his credit, look away. Instead, he studied her shrewdly. "You want too much. Can you guarantee that the mine is as rich as it's reported to be?"

"There're no guarantees in life, Mr. Wyatt. Especially when it comes to treasure hunting. It's all a crapshoot."

"Then you should come down off your price, *Ms.* Brewster. Or at least agree to take less if the mine doesn't have the ore it's rumored to."

"And you should value the fact that you're not going to spend years, possibly decades, looking in the wrong place," she retorted. "Think about it, Mr. Wyatt. Without the right information, you might as well look for the mine in Mexico. You're never going to find it."

She saw his eyes flicker and knew she'd finally scored a direct hit in this game they were playing, but she had to give him credit. He didn't cave in easily. "How do I know that you're not just scamming me?" he asked, studying her with eyes that were sharp as a hawk's. "You've given me no proof, no credentials. For all I know, you're a waitress from Philadelphia. Where's your proof, *Ms.* Brewster? Give me that, and then we'll have something to talk about."

"Well, if that's all you need, why didn't you say so?" she said, and reached into her purse and pulled out a letter.

Chapter 3

Expecting a map of some kind, Buck unfolded the single piece of paper and frowned at the letter that was written in Spanish. "This is your proof?"

"You wanted something in writing."

"Something I could read!"

"You didn't say it had to be in English. Would you like me to translate it for you?"

"Oh, sure. That'll really inspire confidence. Is this all you've got?"

She hesitated, studying him with wary eyes that told him more strongly than words that she didn't trust him any more than he trusted her. That should have done nothing to reassure him. Instead, her wariness told him that she knew something. Why else would she be leery of him?

"You *do* have something else," he said accusingly.

"I do not!"

Her denial was too quick, too fierce. "Yes, you do," he insisted. "I'm not blind. I can see it in your eyes. You're afraid I'm going to take whatever you have and cut you out. And you have every right to feel that way. You don't know me, don't know what I'm capable of. That must be the most difficult part of your job… knowing who to trust. You could lose a bundle before you even knew you were in trouble."

She didn't even bother to deny it. "It happens," she retorted. "Not often, but enough to make me gun-shy. I learned a long time ago not to trust a man who said he wasn't going to take advantage. So if you want me to trust you, Mr. Wyatt, you're going to have to give me something other than words."

He had to give her credit—she didn't pull any punches. Surveying her through narrowed eyes, he started the bidding war. "One percent."

She didn't even blink. "Twenty-five."

Shocked, he laughed. "You can't be serious!"

"Me? What about you? *One percent?* How serious is that?"

"Okay." He chuckled. "So I was testing you, just to see if you were listening."

"Oh, I'm listening," she said dryly. "And your offer is…?"

He had to grin. She was like a dog with a bone. Not, he silently amended, that she in any way resembled a dog. Did she have a clue how cute she was? He'd always been drawn to blondes, but there was something about her black hair and the sparkle of amusement in her blue eyes that he found impossible to ignore. She was sharp as a tack, and he found that incredibly appealing. Did she know that when she smiled, he couldn't take his eyes off her? How was he supposed to negotiate with the woman when he couldn't even think straight around her?

Suddenly realizing where his thoughts had wandered, he stiffened. What the devil was he doing? This was a business deal, for God's sake! If she had the slightest idea what he was thinking, she'd take him to the cleaners in a heartbeat.

Which was why he kept his eyes shuttered as he studied her speculatively. "If you're expecting a lot of money up front for whatever information you think you have, you're out of luck," he said coolly. "The ranch is taking just about every penny I've got, and Hilda, unfortunately, was land rich and dirt poor. There's no money right now for a big payoff."

"And when you find the mine?"

"*If* we find the mine—and that's a big if—then that's another matter, of course."

"So give me a number, Mr. Wyatt. A reasonable number. That's all I ask."

How did he put a price on something he didn't have?

He didn't even know where to start. "If the mine is found, I'll be the one who will bear all the expense."

"True," she agreed. "But without me, you would never find it. You're looking in the wrong place."

"Ten," he said flatly. "It's my last offer."

"Twelve, and you've got a deal," she retorted. "I want twenty-five, you want one. Twelve should work for both of us. Of course, I'm losing out on a half of a percentage point, but that's all right. I'm willing to compromise even if you're not."

Ignoring that last remark, he knew he should have said no and stuck to his offer. After all, he was giving her a hell of a deal, and she should have appreciated that. But no! She wanted more.

And if she didn't get it, she just might walk away.

Scowling, he knew he couldn't let her do that. And it wasn't because she was a damn interesting woman, he assured himself. She knew where the mine was.

"Twelve," he agreed, caving in. "But that's based on net, not gross. And you don't start collecting until six months *after* the mine is up and operating, and that payoff ends after ten years."

"I'm not just turning my notes and maps over to you and walking away for twelve percent or a hundred and five or whatever number you want to throw out there," she told him. "I already informed you I want to be involved in the search for the mine."

"Oh, no!"

"Oh, yes," she insisted. "My father and I spent years

researching the mine, tracking it halfway across the world. I promised my father before he died that I wouldn't stop looking for it. I want to be there when you find it."

He should have said no. She was too cute, too sassy, too hard to ignore. And the last thing he wanted in his life right now was a woman. He'd had one and lost her and he wasn't going there again.

A muscle ticked in his jaw at the thought of Melissa. How could he have been so taken in by her? He'd dated his share of women, and he'd always seen them for what they were…until Melissa looked up at him with those big blue eyes and stole his heart. He'd never seen the mercenary light in those same blue eyes, never realized that she loved what he could give her more than she could ever love him.

Never again, he thought grimly. He didn't need a woman, didn't need another kick in the teeth. He'd welcomed the solitude of the ranch, the time to himself. The last thing he wanted or needed was a woman like Rainey Brewster following him around the ranch, looking for the lost mine and making it impossible for him to ignore her.

But she was the only one who had a clue where the mine was and she wasn't sharing that information unless they had a deal. Damn!

Frustrated, left with no choice, he sighed. "Deal. There. Are you satisfied?"

She didn't even attempt to hold back a triumphant

smile. "Once it's in writing, I will be. So…when do we get started?"

She was serious, he thought with a groan. She was really going to insist on helping him search for the mine. And he'd agreed to the insanity. He must have been out of his mind.

"Eight," he said curtly. "I want to get an early start."

"I'll be there," she assured him, grinning. "You bring the contract, and I'll pack a picnic lunch."

"Just make sure you bring the map," he retorted. "I want to find this damn thing as quickly as possible."

Later, Rainey didn't know how she slept that night. Her thoughts in a whirlwind, she lay in bed for hours, wide awake, her heart racing with excitement, just like a child waiting for Santa Claus. When her father died, she'd given up any real hope of finding the mine—there were so many things that had to come together when you were searching for treasure, and doing it alone wasn't easy. But here she was, so close she could practically reach out and touch it.

If her father had been here, everything would have been perfect. Instead, Buck Wyatt would be at her side, working with her to find the mine.

Her heart stopped in midbeat just at the thought, and that bothered her far more than she liked to admit. The last man who'd stopped her heart that way had also been incredibly good looking and charming. Carl. Just thinking about him tied her stomach in knots. She was eighteen when she met him and had just graduated from high school. He'd wined her and dined her and, worse yet, he'd said all the right things. He'd claimed he hated working in his family's hardware business and couldn't wait for the day when he could quit and join her and her father hunting treasure, and she'd fallen for him—and his story—hook, line and sinker.

He'd lied.

No, she corrected herself. He'd done a hell of a lot more than lie. He'd manipulated her and come close to trapping her in a life he was determined to force on her. He'd never had any intention of leaving the hardware store. Instead, he'd pressured her to give up treasure hunting and stay home and have babies. She wasn't ready for children, and when he promised he would give her time, she thought she could make things work. But the wheels came off the wagon when he not only refused to let her search for a fortune in stolen bank money in Wisconsin, but also washed her birth control pills down the drain with the announcement that he'd decided they were going to have a baby now. She, according to him, didn't get a vote.

He couldn't have been more wrong.

Just thinking about that day still had the power to infuriate her. Outraged that he'd thought he could dictate to her when she had to have a baby, she'd walked out and filed for divorce the very next day. She'd sworn then that she was done with marriage.

Never again, she promised herself. She wasn't setting

herself up for that kind of heartache again. She knew who she was and what she was, and she wasn't letting any man mold her into what he wanted her to be.

But there was something about Buck....

Irritated with herself for even letting that particular thought surface, she drove through the entrance to the Broken Arrow and reminded herself that the only reason she was here was because of the mine. Okay, so Buck was one of those men who could walk into a room full of people and draw the eye of every female in sight. That didn't mean that she intended to give him so much as a second look. She was a professional and planned to stay focused on the treasure. Nothing else mattered.

Her resolve firmly in place, she felt her heart kick into overdrive as she braked to a stop in the circular driveway in front of the house. She had her map, her notes, but she knew it would take more than that to find the mine. The ranch was huge—it covered thousands of acres of trees and canyons and mountains. How much had the landscape changed since the first missionaries arrived and excavated the mine? There must have been earthquakes and landslides and forest fires that forever altered the face of the land. What if everything she found in Spain no longer applied to any section of the ranch? Then what?

Lost in her thoughts, she didn't realize that Buck had opened the front door and was watching her until he stepped over to her VW bug and knocked on her window. Startled, she jumped and glanced up to find him watching her through the window in amusement. "What are you doing?"

"I was just about to ask you the same thing." He chuckled. "You've been sitting there, staring into space for the last ten minutes. If you're having second thoughts about searching for the mine with me, don't feel like you have to. I'll certainly understand if you want to back out. The land's pretty rugged—"

Her chin came up at that. "I've searched for buried treasure all over the world and I haven't had to *back out* of a search yet. Don't worry about me, Mr. Wyatt. I can take care of myself."

"Buck," he reminded her with a knowing smile. "The name's Buck. You don't mind calling me by my first name, do you?"

Just that easily, he put her on the spot. For all of five seconds, she considered admitting that she did have a problem with his request, but she couldn't. Then he would realize that he only had to look at her in a certain way, and she couldn't think straight. Her heart tripped, her breath caught in her throat and she couldn't focus. It was *totally* ridiculous!

Suddenly realizing he was watching every shift in her expression, she stiffened. "Of course I don't mind calling you by your first name, Buck," she said coolly. "Why would I?"

"Why, indeed?" he asked, grinning. Stepping around her car, he opened the door for her. "Now that we have that settled, we need to plan our search. Have you had breakfast? I was waiting for you. We'll go over your notes while we eat. How do you like your eggs?"

"Oh, I don't usually eat breakfast."

"Well, maybe it's time you did," he teased as she followed him into the kitchen. "Now...about those eggs. How'd you say you like them?"

She wasn't really hungry—she was too excited— but it was probably going to be a long day and there was no McDonald's out in the middle of the ranch. "Scrambled," she sighed. "Is there anything I can do to help?"

"Toast," he told her, nodding toward the toaster on the counter near the microwave. "I'll take three. There are also English muffins in the refrigerator, if you like."

Somehow, without quite knowing how it happened, Rainey found herself making breakfast with Buck and feeling as if they'd done it a thousand times before. She was far more intrigued than she liked. There was no question that he knew his way around the kitchen, at least when it came to breakfast. Cracking eggs one-handed, he whisked them with an expert hand, then poured them into the melted butter in a hot skillet before she even had the bread in the toaster.

Where had he learned to cook? she wondered as her gaze wandered freely over his long, lean frame. What woman had stood at his side at a stove and taught him how to crack eggs, how to scramble them so that they were so light and fluffy that they looked like they'd just melt in your mouth? Were they lovers? Had they had late-night cooking lessons after they'd made love? Had he loved her? Did he still?

Why did she care?

His eyes on the eggs he was cooking, he glanced up suddenly and caught her watching him. "What?" he asked, his smile crooked. "The men you date don't cook?"

Heat stung her cheeks, and she looked quickly away. "Actually, I don't date," she retorted stiffly. "I don't have time. But my ex-husband didn't even know where the kitchen was."

"Ah, so you have an ex. Kids?"

"No. How about you?"

"An ex-fiancée," he said flatly. "She broke things off when I moved to America."

Shocked, she blurted out, "Just because you moved? She must not have loved you very much." Too late, she realized what she'd said and quickly apologized. "I'm sorry! I had no right to say that. I don't know the woman. Whatever happened between the two of you is your business."

"Don't apologize," he told her as he carried the skillet of eggs to the kitchen table. "You're right on the money. She'd be here if she really loved me. At the very least, she would have tried to find a compromise. Instead, she handed me my ring back. There was nothing else to discuss."

Suddenly realizing he was telling the details of his private life to a complete stranger, he quickly changed the subject. "Enough of that. Is the toast ready? Let's eat."

* * *

The wooden table that sat before the old rock fireplace at the far end of the kitchen was worn and scarred from use by generations of Wyatts. Taking a seat across from Rainey, the warmth of the morning fire at his back, Buck silently acknowledged that he wasn't a fanciful man. But as he watched Rainey dig into the eggs she really hadn't wanted, he could almost feel his ancestors crowding into the room, hovering close as they waited for word on the whereabouts of the mine.

You're losing it, old chap, he told himself, shaking off his imaginings. There was no such thing as ghosts, and if there were, surely they wouldn't need Rainey Brewster to tell them where the mine was. That kind of thing had to be common knowledge in heaven.

Swallowing a silent groan at that thought—what was he thinking?—he finished his eggs, then sat back in his chair to study her with sharp eyes. "Okay, back to the mine. If it's not near the Indians' summer camp, then where is it?"

"In a canyon that runs east and west," she said promptly, and pulled out the small map she took with her everywhere. "I copied this from the records I discovered in Barcelona. This canyon is where the mine is," she told him, pointing out the canyon that looked like nothing more than a bunch of meaningless lines. "I know it doesn't look like much, but there's a place on this ranch that looks just like this. The Ute Indians considered it haunted. They wouldn't go near it, so the last thing they would have done was camp near it. There's no way the mine is near the Indians' summer camp."

Buck frowned. "The ranch library is full of books about the Utes in this area of Colorado. I don't remember reading anything about a haunted canyon. And I certainly haven't see any canyon on the ranch that looks even vaguely like your map."

"It must be incredibly remote," she replied. "As for any mention of the haunted canyon, I never ran across any reference to it, either," she replied, "until I went to Spain. Maybe they didn't talk about it. It's not uncommon for certain tribes to not speak of their fears of the spirit world. They were a suspicious lot. They would have been afraid of empowering the demons that inhabited such places."

Buck couldn't argue with her logic, but she didn't have a clue how complicated she'd just made their search. "Do you have any idea how many canyons there are on this ranch?" he demanded, frustrated. "There are fifty square miles of them! The mine could be in any one of them. If that's all you've got," he said, motioning to the map she was folding to return to her purse, "then you've made a trip out here for nothing."

"But that's not all," she said when he rose to collect the dishes and carry them to the sink. "There's a stream that hugs the north wall of the canyon."

"There are streams all over the ranch, and they all look alike."

"And there's a bell—"

Frowning, he gave her a sharp look. "What bell?"

"The missionaries brought it with them from Spain."

"Yes, I know," he said. "The Spaniards took it back to Spain after the mine was lost in the landslide. It's in a museum in Madrid."

"No, that's the ship's bell," she corrected him. "The bell that I'm talking about was forged in Italy. The bell in the museum is from Portugal. I know. I've seen it."

There was no doubting her sincerity. "So where's the bell?"

"According to the records in Spain, it never left Colorado," she replied.

"So it was lost in the avalanche."

"There's always that possibility," she agreed, "but I don't think so. According to one missionary's diary, the bell was located a hundred yards due north of the mine's entrance. For all we know, it's still there."

"But you can't be sure of that," he retorted. "So all we have is a rough map of one canyon out of thousands and a bell that may or may not still be there...."

"And a cedar tree at the entrance to the canyon!" she finished for him triumphantly. "The Spaniards wanted to be able to find the mine easily, so they planted one of the cedar trees they brought from Spain to mark the entrance to the canyon. All we have to do is find that tree!"

Buck couldn't believe she was serious. "This is a joke, right?"

"No, of course not," she said automatically, only to turn wary when his question registered. "Why would you think I was joking? Granted, the tree could be dead after all these years, but cedars are hardy—"

"And prolific," he added dryly. "There must be ten thousand on the ranch alone."

She blanched. "Ten *thousand?*"

He nodded. "Possibly more. Cedars love this climate. They sprang up everywhere the wind blew. Haven't you noticed? The canyons and the lower slopes of the foothills are covered with cedar as far as the eye can see."

For a moment, he saw despair spill into her eyes, but just that quickly, she blinked and it was gone. She straightened her shoulders, her chin came up and determination glinted in her eyes. She didn't have to say the words for Buck to know she wasn't giving up. And he was damn impressed. Another woman might have been in tears, but not Rainey Brewster. She looked as if she was ready to take on the world.

"That doesn't mean we can't find it," she said stubbornly. "The bell's got to be somewhere nearby—"

"Not necessarily," he argued. "Someone could have found it years ago and melted it down for bullets or something. Or the Indians could have carried it off. There's no way to know."

"Yes, there is," she insisted. "There are no records of its existence after the landslide. And the Indians wouldn't have come near it because it was in the haunted canyon. It just dropped off the face of the earth. It's got to be there!"

She looked so determined—and desperate—he felt

for her. "Rainey, love, you're looking for a needle in a haystack," he said gently. "You know that, don't you? The odds on finding the mine—"

"Are immaterial," she said promptly. "My father taught me a long time ago that you can't consider the odds when you're looking for lost treasure. That's why other people give up."

Frowning, he said, "I can appreciate your father's philosophy, but at some point, you have to consider the odds and how cost effective your search is—unless you want to spend the rest of your life futilely searching for something and never getting anywhere. When you and I made a deal, I thought you had more information on the mine's location."

"So what are you saying?" she asked, alarmed. "You don't want to search for the mine, after all?"

"You've got very little to go on, Rainey."

"What are you talking about? I have more than I usually do when I start a new search. Think about it. We know it's in a canyon—a haunted canyon, in fact, that runs east and west and has a stream on the north side. An old cedar marks the entrance to the canyon and there is a bell a hundred yards north of the mine's entrance. That's a heck of a lot of clues. And we have a map! What more could you ask for?"

"How about the ghost of one of the dead missionaries to show us the way?" he said dryly.

"You don't have to be sarcastic," she retorted.

"You don't have anything, love!"

"Sometimes, it's the small, seemingly insignificant pieces of information that break a search wide open."

When he looked far from convinced, she added, "I've done this all my life, Buck. And my gut's telling me not to walk away. We have the clues we need to find the mine."

A frown knitting his brows, he studied her consideringly. "No one wants to find the mine more than I do," he finally said. "To be perfectly honest, the ranch is in trouble, and I'm doing everything I can to put it back together. I don't have time to chase after a pipe dream. If you really think you can find the mine, I can give you two weeks. After that, we'll see."

Two weeks wasn't much time to find something that had been lost for centuries, but it was better than nothing. "You've got a deal," she replied promptly. "There is, however, one more thing than you need to know."

"I was wondering when we'd get around to that," he retorted.

Surprised, she eyed him warily. "What?"

"The haunted canyon."

"How did you know I was going to bring that up?"

"Any woman who's spent her life chasing rumors and tall tales has to believe in ghosts and hauntings. How can you not?"

She didn't even try to defend herself. "Guilty as charged," she replied, smiling slightly. "I do believe in ghosts and hauntings and everything else that scares people in the middle of the night. And whether you believe in curses or not, you need to know that the

Indians put a curse on the mine. Anyone who disturbs the mine—and the graves of the dead who died in the avalanche—will risk death themselves."

He just looked at her, humor glinting in his blue eyes. "Tell me you don't really believe that."

She shrugged, a rueful smile curling the corners of her lips. "It's a strange world. I'd rather play it safe than sorry."

"Then I guess that's the difference between me and you," he said. "Because, curse or no curse, if we can narrow down where the mine is, I'll turn over every rock on this ranch to find it."

When he headed for the back door, Rainey never moved. Surprised, he glanced over his shoulder and frowned. "Have you changed your mind? I've got the Jeep out back. I thought we'd work our way north of the house, then circle back around to the east."

"I have a better way," she told him. "Come with me."

He took one look at the mischief dancing in her eyes and should have said, *Thanks, but no thanks.* Any man with brains in his head knew better than to trust a woman with that kind of look in her eye. Curiosity, however, got the better of him.

Eyeing her warily, he took a step toward her and said, "Why do I have the feeling I'm going to regret this?"

She laughed. "No guts, no glory, Mr. Wyatt. Are you in or out?"

This was his chance. He should have said no, at least until he knew what she was up to, but he'd never been one to step back from a challenge. "I'm in," he growled.

Chapter 4

The airfield on the north end of town was nothing more than a mowed pasture that served as a landing strip. There was no tower, no lights, only a fuel tank where the local ranchers could fill up their planes and a flag to denote the direction of the wind.

When Rainey pulled into the airfield parking lot, Buck looked at her in surprise. "What are we doing here?"

"Going up," she replied with a smile. "We need to get an aerial view of the ranch and chart the canyon, so I rented a plane. It wasn't that expensive, and it'll save us a lot of time in the long run."

"You hired a pilot?"

"No. I have my license."

He just looked at her. "You can't be serious."

Rainey laughed at his tone. "Of course I'm serious," she said as she cut the engine and stepped from the car. "I've had my license for years. It comes in handy when I'm working in the middle of nowhere."

When he joined her in front of the plane and hesitated, she struggled not to smile. "Is something wrong? You're not afraid of flying in small planes, are you?"

"Oh, no!"

"Or women pilots?"

"Of course not!"

He spoke quickly…too quickly, but she couldn't take offense. From what she had seen of Buck Wyatt, he was the kind of man who liked to be in charge. Putting his life in someone else's hands, especially a woman's, wouldn't be easy for him.

"I'm a good pilot, Buck," she assured him. "I know what I'm doing. There's nothing to worry about."

"I didn't say I was worried," he retorted. "I'm just not stepping into that plane until I see your license."

Grinning, she pulled her license out of her purse. "There. Satisfied?"

"I'll tell you when we're back on the ground," he said and followed her into the plane.

"You're a sadist," he yelled at her over the sound of the motor as Rainey banked the plane and sent the Cessna circling back to the west. His stomach nose-dived, and with a muttered curse, Buck hung on for dear life. "You're going to pay for this!"

"Wah!" She laughed. "What a baby."

"You'll think baby," he warned. "Watch the trees. You're too low!"

Chuckling, she eased back on the throttle, lifting them well above the treetops. "You really do need to lighten up. We're perfectly safe, Buck. I'm just trying to get a good view of the canyons."

His jaw clenched on an oath, he never took his eyes off the scene in front of them. "We can see the canyons just fine at a higher altitude. All you can see is trees, anyway."

Her gaze following his, Rainey had to agree. The trees were much thicker than she'd expected. "What about creeks or streams? What about there?" she said, nodding toward the canyon to the east that hugged the base of the mountains. "Is that a dry creek bed running between the trees?"

Frowning, he leaned forward to get a better look. "It's a creek bed, all right, but the canyon runs north and south. Damn!"

One canyon led to another, however, and they soon came across dozens of canyons that ran east and west. "Do you see anything that looks like the remains of an avalanche?" she asked as she buzzed low over each canyon. "There's got to be something."

"Not so far," he said grimly. "I told you this wasn't going to be easy."

"I know," she agreed, "but at least we've eliminated some of the canyons and narrowed the search. That's all we can do from the air."

"Now that I've seen some of these canyons from the air, I don't know that we're going to be able to do much from the ground, either," he warned. "They're pretty damn rugged."

"Don't you have a Jeep? We can go off-roading as much as we can, then do the rest on foot," she assured him. Shooting him a quick look as she headed back to the airstrip, she said, "So when do you want to go into the canyons?"

"How does three o'clock sound?" he replied.

"Three o'clock? This afternoon? It's a quarter to three now!"

Grinning, he nodded. "There's no use wasting time. If we get started as soon as we get back to the ranch, we'll still have time to check out at least a few of the canyons today. It's a start, anyway."

"What about your foreman?" she asked with a frown. "Is he the type to go into town and talk about the two of us searching for the mine?"

"David?" He chuckled. "Not likely. He's pretty close mouthed. He doesn't even talk to me except about work, so don't worry. He's not going to say much. Anyway, all he's going to know is that I'm just showing you around the ranch. There's no reason for him or anyone else to suspect we're looking for the mine...unless, of course, you told someone in town your real reason for being here."

"You don't have to worry about that," she assured him. "I haven't told a soul. I learned a long time ago not to talk about my job or what I was after. As far as anyone in town knows, I'm here to research a book on the Wyatt family and their place in Colorado history."

"So no one will be suspicious if you're seen talking to me," he said, impressed, "or spending the next two weeks going over the Broken Arrow with a fine-tooth comb."

"Exactly," she said with a grin. "I'm just doing research."

"Clever girl."

Her blue eyes twinkling, she shrugged. "It works for me."

"Then let's go do some research," he suggested, "and see what we can find."

When David brought the Jeep around for them, Buck introduced Rainey to him, and said easily, "Rainey's doing a book on the ranch, so you're going to be seeing a lot of her over the next couple of weeks. I'm going to take her to the Indian summer camp, then drive her up into the mountains."

"Have him take you to the old hunting cabin," David told her as they shook hands. "There's a great view from up there and you might even see a few elk if you're lucky."

"That would be wonderful," Rainey told him. "I've been reading about the ranch for years and can't wait to see everything. There's a family cemetery, isn't there? Joshua Wyatt is buried there? I read that it's in a stand of aspens that are incredible in the fall."

David nodded. "I've only been working here since January, so I haven't seen it in the fall, but it is in a stand of aspens. It's very peaceful."

"Maybe we'll go there first," Buck said. "Since Joshua settled the ranch, it seems appropriate to start there."

"Watch the brakes," David warned him. "I put on new pads—they're a little touchy."

"I'll be careful," he assured him. "We'll see you later."

Her heart thumping with excitement, Rainey expected Buck to head for the northwest corner of the ranch, to the area they'd flown over earlier, but he headed straight west, instead, toward the snowcapped mountains in the distance.

Surprised, she arched a brow at him. "We're going to the cemetery?"

"I wasn't just trying to mislead David," he said quietly. "It seems like the right place to start."

"I agree. I've been reading about the Broken Arrow and the Wyatts for so long that I feel like I know your ancestors as well as I know my own. I would love to see the cemetery."

"It was one of the first places I visited when I arrived at the ranch," he said. "There was snow everywhere and I needed a four-wheel drive to get there, but it was worth the trip. The second I stepped into the cemetery and saw the old headstones with my family name, I knew I was where I belonged. Where I'd always belonged."

With nothing more than those simple words, he stirred a longing in her that she usually kept buried deep in her heart. "I've never had a place like that," she said quietly. "That must be an incredible feeling."

"It is," he agreed. "What about when you were married? You must have felt some kind of contentment with your husband. I know the two of you divorced, but surely, when you were first married and had your own place, you must have felt like you were home."

"You would think," she agreed. "But it was never like that, not even from the beginning. That should have told me something, but I was young and naive, and trying to make it work. It never did."

"Why?" he asked, only to put a hand up, stopping her. "I'm sorry. I really shouldn't have asked that. It's private—"

"It's ancient history," she countered. "It doesn't hurt like it used to, probably because I *did* get out of a situation that was all wrong for me. Carl wanted a *yes, dear* wife."

She didn't have to explain. He grinned. "That's not you."

"Not even at eighteen," she agreed. "He wanted me to stay home and have babies and let him decide what our life was going to be like. Of course, he failed to mention any of that when we were dating."

"When did you realize the man you married was not the one you fell in love with?"

"About a month after we got married," she admitted. "He convinced me that I needed to stay home and work in his family's hardware store instead of going with my father."

"Asking a wife to stay home with her husband isn't an unreasonable request," he pointed out.

"It is if the husband promised to quit his job with his family and join his wife's business before they married, then reneged on that promise," she argued.

She told him everything then, including how Carl informed her that he was the one who got to decide when *she* was going to get pregnant. "That was the straw that broke the camel's back," she said bluntly. "I was done."

"So you went back to your dad?"

"No, actually, I went to college, then graduate school, then—"

"You got your Ph.D.," he finished for her, grinning. "So you weren't lying about that on your business card."

"Lying? Of course not! Why would you think that?"

He shrugged, his grin deepening. "You're a treasure hunter, Rainey. An adventurer. There's bound to be a lot of con men in your line of work."

Far from offended, she only laughed. "You got that right. I could tell you stories that would curl your hair."

"I'm sure you could," he chuckled. "So is that why you got the degree? So people would take you more seriously?"

"Partly. But I also love history. Once I started college, I just couldn't seem to stop learning. And my dad encouraged me. He never had a chance to go to college and he wanted me to go as far as I could."

"You know, you could be using that doctorate to make a heck of a lot more than you are, don't you?"

"Don't be too sure of that," she said with a grin. "I'm damn good at what I do. And when we find the mine, I may never have to work again."

"Me, neither," he quipped, chuckling, as he turned off into the trees. "If—"

"Don't say if! We're going to find it."

He parked in front of the old-fashioned iron fence that surrounded the cemetery. Turning off the engine, he smiled ruefully. "Time will tell. Come and meet the family."

Rainey had been to her share of cemeteries—she loved the history told on tombstones—and she thought she knew what to expect. But when she walked through the gate into the Wyatt-family cemetery, the peace that settled over her caught her off guard. She tried to tell herself it was the aspens—they seemed to whisper in the soft breeze, telling stories of the past—or the mountains that stood sentinel over the graves, forever watchful, but it was more than that. It was something she couldn't put a name to, something that brought the sting of tears to her eyes and shook her to her core at one and the same time.

"Well?"

She didn't realize he was watching her until she looked up at his quiet question and found his eyes on her. For reasons she couldn't explain, her heart beat faster, surprising her. What was he asking her and why did she feel as if she knew the answer?

"It's beautiful," she said quickly, dragging her eyes from his to look around. "It says everything about the ranch you need to know. It's your roots. It doesn't matter that you weren't born here or that you never met any of these people. This is where you came from, where your children and grandchildren will come from. It's who you are."

Surprised, he blinked. "How did you know that's the way I felt?"

"It's what we're all looking for," she said simply. "Something that connects us to each other, to the land itself. When you're lucky enough to find it, you know it. And you fight to hang on to it with everything you've got."

In just a few words, she'd completely summed up how he felt about the ranch. How had she understood so quickly? "You know, you're pretty smart for a Yank," he said with a grin. "Let's go see if you're smart enough to find the mine."

"Oh, I'm smart enough," she retorted with twinkling eyes. "All I need is enough time, and I can find anything. Which way are the canyons from here?"

"That way," he said, nodding to the northwest as they headed back to the Jeep. "I'll have you there in no time."

They drove toward the mountains and had gone little more than a mile when he warned her, "Hold on!"

And before she could guess his intentions, he turned off the ranch road and struck off through the trees, bouncing over the rough terrain without once checking his speed. Laughing, she grabbed on to her armrest and the dash. "Whoa! Slow down!"

He laughed. "Can't. Not if we want to check any canyons before dark. Uh-oh. Watch it!"

He hit the low-lying stream without ever slowing down, sending the cold clear water up into the air. Protected by the Jeep's soft canvas top and sides, Rainey knew she was in no danger of getting wet, but she instinctively ducked anyway.

"What are you ducking for?" he said. "It's just water."

Trying to frown and failing miserably, she said, "Has anyone told you you're crazy? You talk about my flying—what about your driving? At least I don't play tag with a bunch of trees. Do you even know where you're going?"

"Of course—"

"Oh, God! Look out!"

If his reflexes hadn't been lightning quick as he darted around a stand of ancient firs, Buck would have driven right off a small cliff into a dry creek bed. Swearing, he jerked the wheel hard to the left and hit the brakes as the Jeep skidded and bucked and just missed several massive trees by mere inches. Then, with no warning, the brake pedal went all the way to the floorboard.

"What the hell!"

"What?" Rainey asked, alarmed. "What's wrong?"

"No brakes," he said through his teeth as he fought to control the Jeep before they slammed into a tree. "Hang on."

Hang on! she thought wildly. Couldn't he see that she was already holding on for dear life? And it wasn't helping! Trees whizzed past them and her life flashed before her eyes. She wanted to scream, to jump clear, to stomp on the brake and try to bring the Jeep to a stop, but there was nothing she could do.

Then, almost as soon as their wild ride began, it was over. They reached the bottom of the hill they were racing down and started up the next one and immediately began to slow down. As the Jeep slowed to a crawl, Buck turned it into the trees before they could start to roll backward and brought it to a shuddering stop.

How long they both sat there, stunned, neither could have said. Rainey was the first to blink. "Well," she said, expelling her breath in a long, shaky sigh, "that was a heck of a ride. I take back everything I said about you driving on the wrong side of the road. You were incredible."

"That was too damn close," he growled. "What the blazes happened to the brakes?"

"Didn't David say he just put on new brake pads?"

"He sure as hell did," he said grimly. "Either he was lying or he didn't know what he was doing. Either way, he's got a lot of explaining to do. We could have been killed."

"We would have been if your reflexes hadn't been so good," she replied. "So now what? Obviously, we can't drive back to the house, so I guess that means—"

"We walk," he finished for her. "And we don't have time to dally. It'll be dark soon."

The sun was already on its downward slant, and the shadows were growing long. Once it slipped behind the mountains, darkness would spread quickly and they were a long way from the homestead. "Lead the way," she said, and jumped out of the Jeep.

He turned back the way they had come and she quickly fell into step beside him. "We probably wouldn't have made it to the canyons anyway," she said as they started up the hill they'd come careening down only a few minutes before. "We started too late."

His lips twitched. "So what are you saying? Fate played with our brakes so we wouldn't make a wasted trip and get lost in the canyons after dark?"

"You don't believe in fate?"

At her arch look, he grinned. "Oh, no. I believe in it—I wouldn't be here if it hadn't stepped into my life."

"Me, neither," she chuckled. "Some things are just meant to be."

"I guess your psychic told you that."

Even in the fading light, she could see the teasing glint in his eyes. "You know, that's the second time you've mentioned psychics. How can you believe in fate, but not psychics?"

"Because one's an unseen force in the world and the other one's a scam artist."

"There are some good ones out there."

"Yeah, right. So what'd they tell you? You were going to meet some tall, dark and handsome man and you'd live happily every after? Tell me you didn't fall for that."

Arching a brow at him, she smiled. "You don't believe in happily-ever-after?"

"Nope. The women I've known only stay in love as long as everything goes their way. The second things don't, they're history. But we weren't talking about me," he reminded her. "So, when are you supposed to meet Mr. Tall, Dark and Handsome?"

"Did I mention that I wasn't looking for a man?"

"You're avoiding the question, so obviously somebody read your palm and said something that struck a nerve. Who was she? Some Gypsy in Eastern Europe? A voodoo queen in New Orleans? Come on—give. You may as well tell me, you know. We've got a long walk ahead of us and I'm going to hound the hell out of you until you tell me."

She should have told him to stuff it, but she only had to look into his eyes to know that he wasn't going to let this go. It would, she thought in amusement, serve him right if she told him a psychic had told her she would lose her heart to a man with a British accent. Instead, she told him the truth.

"She was a psychic in Budapest," she admitted. "I was sixteen, and on a treasure hunt with my father. She told me I was going to meet a man with an old name and old money. One side of his family would welcome me with open arms. The other would do everything they could to drive me away."

Startled, he blinked. "No kidding? Did your ex's family resent you?"

"They knew I didn't want to work at the hardware store—or stay home, for that matter. Carl's mother made no secret of the fact that she thought I was all wrong for her son."

"That could fit," he agreed. "So who welcomed you with open arms?"

"No one."

"There you go. That's the problem with psychics. People twist and turn things to try to make the psychic's prediction come true when they're probably dead wrong to begin with. I'll bet you haven't even met the man the psychic was talking about."

"Then I'm never going to meet him," she retorted. "Once was enough. If I haven't met him, then he'll have to wait until our next lifetime. I'm done. Been there, done that. I have absolutely no interest in making that mistake again. Once was enough."

"I know what you mean," he said. "When Melissa gave me my ring back, you could have knocked me over with a feather. Talk about feeling loved. That did it for me."

"Do you regret coming to Colorado?" she asked, curious. "You might be able to win her back if you went back to London."

"If she really loved me, she'd love me regardless of where I lived. No, I won't be going back to London," he said firmly. "At least, not anytime soon, and when I do, I won't be looking up Melissa."

Stopping abruptly as they reached the top of the hill, he frowned at the ranch road, which was barely discernible in the fading light. It wound through the lower foothills of the mountains, disappearing through the trees, only to reappear in the open areas on its way back to the homestead.

"What's wrong?" Rainey asked quietly. "Why'd you stop?"

"It's going to take forever to get back to the house if we stick to the road. I think we should cut across country. It's a straight shot to the house, and it'll save us at least five miles."

"Can you find your way in the dark?"

He nodded. "I carry a compass with me wherever I go on the ranch. And it lights up in the dark. We just have to keep going southeast."

"I'm game if you are," she said. "Let's go."

He held out his hand to her. "Give me your hand."

Surprised, she frowned. "Why?"

"Because I don't want to lose you in the dark. C'mon," he teased, "don't be a baby. Any minute now, it's going to get damn dark. We need to stick together."

He had a point. It was getting dark very quickly and her night vision wasn't the best. Her heart pounding, she slipped her hand into his.

Almost immediately, she knew it was a mistake. His fingers closed around hers and she felt…safe. She should have snatched her hand back, should have come up with some kind of excuse. But she couldn't. Not yet.

"Watch your step," he growled, and struck off through the trees with her in tow.

They headed southeast, and for a while they made good time. Then the darkness became complete and their pace slowed considerably. "This is my fault," Buck said. "We should have waited until tomorrow morning to do this. Feel free to tell me *I told you so* at any time."

He sounded so disgusted, she had to laugh. "Will you relax? You didn't know the brakes were going to go on the Jeep and we'd have to walk back. And it's no big deal, anyway. It's not like we're in the wilds of the Amazon and worried about being some jaguar's dinner. We're on your ranch!"

He knew she was right, but as he kept one eye on the compass and the other on the trees he was carefully guiding them through, they seemed farther away from the homestead than ever. Then they topped a hill and there on the horizon was a faint glow.

"It could be the moon," she warned.

"It's a light," he said. "That's good enough for me."

They headed straight for the horizon, but the going wasn't easy. Trees and dead timber, not to mention rocks, seemed to jump out of the darkness when they least expected it. Trying to keep up, Rainey never saw the rotten log that blended into the dark shadows at her feet and reached out to trip her.

It happened so quickly, she didn't have time to do anything but gasp. Then, in the next instant, Buck's fingers tightened around hers and he caught her before she could even think about falling.

Her heart thundering in her breast, she told herself she was suddenly breathless because she'd almost landed face-first in the dirt. It had nothing to do with

Buck…or the fact that his fingers were wrapped around hers like he would never let her go.

"You know, we're never going to make it to the house if you don't stop throwing yourself at me," he said teasingly. "I know I'm hard to resist, but where's your pride?"

"I was just asking myself the same thing," she quipped breathlessly, and prayed he didn't realize she was serious. Where *was* her pride? What was wrong with her? How could he make her forget she wasn't looking for a man just by taking her hand in his?

"Are you all right?" he asked gruffly.

"Of course," she replied, and knew nothing could have been further from the truth. The man was getting under her skin, and there didn't seem to be a damn thing she could do about it.

When they finally broke through the trees and saw the lighted compound of the homestead ahead of them, Rainey didn't know if she wanted to laugh or cry. "Is that— ?"

"My God, it is! I was beginning to wonder if we were going to stumble around out here all night."

"We came close," she said. "It's nearly midnight. We've been walking for hours!"

"And this was the shortcut," he said. "No wonder I'm starving. It's been a long time since breakfast."

Rainey laughed. "I know what you mean. I passed hungry a long time ago. The next time we get lost—"

"We weren't—"

"Lost," she finished for him, chuckling. "Yes, I know. Okay, then, the next time we misplace the homestead, remind me to bring enough food for a couple of days. Just in case."

He grinned. "A couple of days, huh? Sounds like you're intending to get stranded with me again."

"We weren't stranded."

"If you wanted to run away together, you should have just said so. I'm an accommodating kind of guy, love. And I like a woman who knows what she wants."

He was pushing her buttons—and doing a damn good job of it—but she only smiled slightly, ran her eyes over him as they stepped out of the darkness into the light and shrugged. "When I see something I like, I'll let you know."

He gave a shout of laughter. "You do that, love. In the meantime, let's go cook up something hot for dinner. If you cook, I'll do the dishes."

There was nothing she wanted more—and for no other reason than that she knew she couldn't stay. "I'd love to," she said, "but it's late, and I'm really tired. Can I take a rain check?"

For a moment, she thought he was going to try to change her mind, but he obviously thought better of it. "Of course," he said easily. "I need to track David down anyway and get an explanation about that damn brake job he did on the Jeep."

He escorted her to the front door, only to frown when he saw how tired she looked. "Are you sure you feel like driving back to the motel? It's been a long day and you look beat."

"I'm fine. Really."

"You're ready to fall on your face and you know it," he retorted. "Why don't you leave your car here and let me drive you back?"

"But how would I get my car?"

"I'll pick you up in the morning."

"But the Jeep's out of commission," she reminded him. "We can't start the search again until it's fixed—unless you have another vehicle."

"We've got the pickup," he said, "but you're right. David and I will have to tow the Jeep back to the house, then find out what went wrong with the brakes."

"So it's better if I drive myself back to the motel," she said. It's only a fifteen-minute drive. I'll be fine."

Resigned, he reluctantly agreed. "All right, have it your way. Just call me when you get home so I know you made it. Okay?"

"Of course," she said easily as he opened the driver's door for her. She started to slip into the seat, only to hesitate. "I really did have a good time today," she told him with a grin. "Even if you did get us lost."

"I didn't—"

"Of course you did." She chuckled. "Not that I expect you to admit it."

"Good! Then you're not disappointed."

"I know men have a hard time making that kind of admission," she continued as if he hadn't spoken. "It must be something in your DNA, because women aren't like that. We ask directions. And we can certainly admit when we made a mistake—"

"Really?" he growled, grinning. "So my DNA's at fault, is it? Well, let me show you something else that's in my genes." And with no other warning than that, he pulled her into his arms.

Chapter 5

Caught off guard, she didn't have time to think, to breathe, to do anything but feel. Her head spinning, her heart pounding, she felt herself start to melt into his arms and couldn't seem to do anything about it. How could he do this to her so easily? She barely knew him. Yet he only had to touch her, kiss her, and she totally lost her head.

Dizzy, her thoughts clouding, she knew she had to do something fast or she was going to do something foolish…like give in to the aching need he stirred in her so effortlessly. If she had an ounce of sense, she'd just step out of his arms.

It should have been easy. All she had to do was take a single step back, and she would have been free. But how could she when he deepened the kiss and all she wanted to do was kiss him back? Just for a moment, she promised herself. He'd been holding her hand for hours, teasing her, somehow turning their time together into a date with just his touch, and all she wanted was just this one kiss, then she would come to her senses.

But one second slipped into another, then another, and the moment she craved threatened to stretch into an eternity. She was on the verge of forgetting her own name when she suddenly realized she was plastered all over the man.

Breathless, her heart slamming against her ribs, she abruptly stepped back. "I—I have to g-go."

"Rainey—wait!"

"Call me tomorrow after you deal with the Jeep and let me know when we can start the search. Good night." And not giving him time to say another word, she drove off like the hounds of hell were after her.

Later, she didn't even remember the drive back to Willow Bend. Her thoughts in a whirl, all she could think of was Buck and a kiss that had gone on and on and on. She could still taste him on her tongue, still feel him against her. What was she thinking? What was *he* thinking? She must have been out of her mind. That was the only explanation. What other reason could she have for kissing the man like that?

Idiot! She knew better. Buck Wyatt was off limits— they had a business arrangement, for heaven's sake! And she wasn't looking for love or romance or even sex.

Especially with a man like Buck. He was too…sexy, too good looking, too…sensual. He only had to look at her with those bedroom eyes of his, and she completely forgot about the mine and why she was there. She had two weeks, that was it, before she had to move on to another treasure. When she left, she wasn't leaving her heart behind.

Caught up in her thoughts, she made the drive to Willow Bend in record time and wasn't surprised to find the place closed up like a ghost town. At least they didn't roll up the sidewalks, she thought as she arrived at her motel and drove around to the back of the building to her room. Not that anyone was out walking at midnight. The only living thing in sight was the cat inspecting the motel Dumpster in the far corner of the parking lot.

The motel was far from full, so she was able to get a parking space right in front of her room. Pleased, she was digging for her room key as she approached her door when something—a sixth sense—set her internal alarm bells screeching like a banshee. Stopping abruptly, she looked up sharply.

The night was quiet—there wasn't even a breeze to ruffle the pine needles in the trees—and the parking lot was well lit. She was alone but for the cat in the Dumpster, and there wasn't any visible reason to be alarmed. Every ounce of self-preservation she possessed, however, told her something was wrong.

Her heart in her throat, fighting the need to run for

cover, she stood perfectly still—only her eyes moved as she checked out her surroundings. There were four cars, including hers, parked in front of rooms, and they all appeared to be empty and locked. The drapes were drawn across the windows of all the rooms, the doors shut—

The door to her room was open a crack.

Horrified, her eyes locked on the sliver of space between the door and the jamb. She was three steps from the door and couldn't have moved if her life had depended on it. Had she locked it? She would have sworn she had, but she'd been so excited about looking for the mine when she left that she might not have pulled the door completely shut.

Then again, maybe the maid had been careless, she reasoned, desperately searching for answers. She could have been distracted, had her hands full…there were any number of reasons why the door might have been accidentally left ajar. That didn't mean a burglar had broken in—or was still in there.

So why were the fine hairs on the back of her neck tingling in alarm?

Later, she didn't remember moving, but the next thing she knew, she was back in her car with all the doors locked. Lightning quick, without even thinking, she called Buck. It wasn't until she heard his voice on the other end of the line that she realized she had his number memorized.

"Hello?"

"Buck? I—"

"Good. You got home safely. I was afraid you'd forget to call."

"My room—"

That was all she managed to say, just those two words, but he must have heard something in her voice that alarmed him. "What's wrong? Are you all right?"

"The door to my room's open. I—"

"Don't go in! I'll be right there!"

"Wait!"

The line went dead, and she didn't know his cell number. Suddenly chilled to the bone, she hugged herself and never took her eyes off the door to her motel room.

The sheriff and his men arrived within minutes. Only then did she feel safe enough to unlock her car door and step out on the sidewalk. "How—"

"We got a call that you might have an intruder," the uniformed police officer said. "I'm Officer Tucker. Are you Rainey Brewster?"

She nodded. "The door to my room's open a crack—"

"Stay right here," he said gruffly. "I'll check it out."

Standing to the left of the door, he knocked sharply on the doorjamb. "Police! Open up!"

The door didn't move so much as an inch, and there was no response to the officer's order. In the tense silence, the whisper-soft sound of his gun being drawn was deafening.

Alarmed, Rainey only had time to jump for cover when the policeman suddenly kicked open the door and slammed it against the motel-room wall. Even from where she stood, she could see that her room had been turned upside down. The mattress was half off the bed, the sheets and bedspread in disarray, but that didn't alarm her nearly as much as the sight of her ransacked suitcase lying on the floor, with her things scattered everywhere.

"Oh my God!"

Horrified, she stepped forward instinctively, but the sheriff immediately stepped in front of her, blocking her path. "Not so fast, ma'am," he said quickly. "It's not safe yet—whoever broke in could still be in there. And even if he's not, it's going to be a while before you can go inside. It's a crime scene. We have to check for evidence."

The words were hardly out of his mouth when a green pickup came racing around the corner of the building, its headlights cutting a wide swath in the darkness and immediately illuminating where she stood outside her room with the sheriff. It wasn't until the driver braked to a stop right next to them that she realized it was Buck.

"Are you all right?" he asked her worriedly.

Up until that moment, she'd been nervous, but generally in control of her emotions. Fear wasn't something she usually gave in to—she worked in a field in which one or more people were after the same treasure she was, and this wasn't the first time her room had been ransacked. She'd learned a long time ago to keep her laptop and any research papers with her at all times, so she didn't generally get rattled. But she hadn't told anyone but Buck why she was in town. Who was watching her? And how did they know what she was after?

It was awfully early in the game for such shenanigans, she thought with a frown, and she didn't mind admitting that she was concerned. She'd been in the treasure-hunting business a long time—she knew all the players, who was better at the game than others, who would stoop to just about anything to grab the treasure and run with it. And she hadn't seen a single one of her cohorts anywhere. So who broke into her room?

"Rainey?"

Coming back to her surroundings with a blink, she glanced up to find Buck studying her with growing concern. She knew what he was thinking—the same thing she was. *This had to have something to do with the mine. Why else would someone search her room?* "Sorry. I'm just a little unnerved."

He reached for her then, and she didn't realize how much she needed him to hold her until his arms closed around her. Later, she knew that was going to keep her awake long into the night, but for the moment, she couldn't be concerned about that. She was just glad he was there.

Holding her close, he scowled at the sheriff. "What happened?"

At his growl, Sherm Clark could only shrug. "Someone broke in and trashed her room. I was working late at the office and heard the call come in on the radio, so

I thought I'd come over and see if Tucker could use some help."

"Whoever was here is long gone," Officer Tucker announced as he stepped outside, slipping his gun back into his holster. Training a sharp eye on Rainey, he said, "Any idea who may have done this, ma'am?"

"None," she said honestly as she stepped out of Buck's arms to survey her ransacked room from the doorway. "Mr. Wyatt is the only one I know in town, and I know he didn't do it. We were together all day."

"What I want to know is how the bugger got in," Buck said, surveying the door to her room critically. "It doesn't look like the lock was forced."

"I agree." Turning his attention back to Rainey, Tucker lifted a dark brow at her. "Did you lock your door, ma'am? Or give anyone your key?"

"No, of course not! I mean, yes, I locked it. Of course I did. And my room key hasn't been out of my possession since I checked in. Maybe the maid forgot to pull the door completely closed."

"I'll check with the front office," the sheriff said, "but chances are, she closed it. She wouldn't keep her job very long if she made a habit of not locking doors after she cleaned the rooms."

"Then maybe someone found a way to steal the passkey from the office, or from the maid," she said stubbornly. "I don't how someone got in, but I know I locked my door."

"As soon as we check for prints, we'll need you to go

through your things and see if anything is missing," Officer Tucker said, stepping in before the sheriff could argue further. "Did you leave any valuables unattended?"

"No," she sighed. "Just my clothes, and I doubt that anyone would take them."

Her notes on the mine, however, were another matter. She could name a half-dozen or more fortune hunters who would love to get their hands on them, but if they were responsible for the break-in, they'd wasted their time. Her notes were well hidden and she took them with her wherever she went. That, however, was something she had no intention of mentioning to the police or anyone else.

Waiting until the sheriff and Officer Tucker had returned to their investigative duties, Buck said quietly, "Okay, level with me. This is about the mine, isn't it?"

Never taking her eyes off the open door to her room, where she could see Officer Tucker dusting for fingerprints, she murmured, "I think it's a good possibility. I don't have anything else that anyone would be interested in."

"So who do you think did this? One of your competitors? Who knows you're here?"

"That's the problem," she admitted huskily. "No one that I can think of."

Surprised, Buck stepped in front of her, blocking Tucker's view of their conversation. "Are you saying that you don't have a clue who might have done this?"

"Oh, I know a few people who wouldn't hesitate

to go to these lengths to get their hands on my notes, but right now, every single one of them is overseas. And as far as I know, none of them have a clue that I'm in Colorado."

His expression grim, Buck turned to survey her trashed room with hard eyes. "Damn, I hate to hear that."

"Why do you say that?"

"Because if you don't know anyone who could have done this, that means it's someone local."

"Who's after my notes?" she asked, surprised. "How would they know about them?"

"I don't know," he retorted, "but look at it this way. Everyone in Willow Bend not only knows everyone else, they know their family and friends, who's in debt, who smokes pot and plays around on their wives. And there are only two strangers in town—you and me. They know why I'm here—to inherit the ranch—and believe me, there are a lot of people who aren't happy about that. Then you show up in town, start hanging out with me, and suddenly your room is ransacked. Somebody's trying to figure out why you're here or they're looking for your notes or trying to scare you off."

"Or all of the above," she added. "I don't scare off that easily."

The words were hardly out of her mouth when Officer Tucker stepped out of her room and said, "Okay, Ms. Brewster, I need you to check to see if anything's missing from your room."

"Of course," she said, turning to join him at the

doorway. "I don't have anything but my suitcase and my clothes, but I'll check."

"Did you find any fingerprints?" Buck asked the officer as Rainey stepped into her room.

"Only a couple," he said, "but I wouldn't be surprised if they turned out to be Ms. Brewster's or the maid's...especially since there was no forced entry."

"You think the maid left the door ajar and the wind blew it open? Even if by some wild quirk of nature that happened, that still doesn't explain who trashed Ms. Brewster's room and why."

"It could have been teenagers—"

"Or the Easter Bunny," Buck growled. "That's bull and you know it."

Tucker shot him a sharp look. "Do you have a better explanation, Mr. Wyatt?"

"That's pretty damn obvious," he retorted. "Whoever did this had a key. You need to question everyone, from the motel staff to the guests. Someone's bound to know something."

"The staff isn't that large," the sheriff said, joining them. "I talked to the clerk at the front desk. One of the maids found Ms. Brewster's key in the parking lot outside her room. It must have fallen out of her purse when she left earlier."

"It couldn't have," she said, frowning in confusion as she stepped out of her room to join them. "I remember putting it back in my purse—"

Holding out the key to her, he lifted a mocking

brow. "Really? Then how do you explain this? I believe it's yours."

In the process of checking her purse, Rainey glanced up and couldn't deny that the old-fashioned room key was hers. It had her room number clearly stamped on it. "This makes no sense. I dropped the key into the bottom of my purse. You can see how heavy it is. There's no way it could have fallen out."

"Did you set your purse down anywhere?" Buck asked. "Could someone have gotten access to the key when your back was turned?"

"Absolutely not," she insisted. "I always keep my purse with me."

"Then you dropped the key when you thought you put it in your purse," the sheriff said flatly. "There's been a gang of teenagers on the tear around here for the last couple of weeks, and I would bet they found the key and decided to check out your room."

"And they were smart enough to make sure there were no witnesses? There weren't any, were there?"

"No," he said stiffly. "The clerk didn't see or hear anything, and there're only two other guests registered to rooms on the back side of the motel. I questioned both of them. They didn't hear anything."

"Come on, Sheriff. Do you really think a gang of teenagers could be that quiet?" Buck demanded. "Get serious."

"They've done similar things," Officer Tucker added. "They've been terrorizing the town and the roads, and we haven't had much luck catching them."

"So that's it?" Buck demanded. "The teenagers did it? End of story? What do you expect Ms. Brewster to do? Clean up her room and act like nothing happened?"

"Without any witnesses, there's not much we can do," the sheriff retorted. "Tucker will run the prints through the state crime lab and wait to see if there are any matches. If there aren't any, there's not a hell of a lot we can do unless someone comes forward as a witness. And you need to know the odds on that are slim to none."

"Then there's nothing else to say," Rainey said quietly. "Thank you for your help, gentlemen. I'll be fine."

"Call us if you need us," the sheriff told her. "Good night."

Disgusted, Buck waited only until the two law enforcement officers were in their vehicles and driving away before he swore. "That's a load of bull—"

"Kids didn't do this, Buck."

"I know that," he said flatly, "but there was no convincing them of that. Are you sure you didn't set your purse down somewhere? At the gas station? Or maybe even here at the motel? Did you make a trip to the ice machine before you left and leave your door open? Anything that would have given someone access to your purse?"

"No, nothing."

"Okay, you had the key yesterday. What about today, before you came to the house? Did you do anything before you came to the ranch?"

"No. Wait!" She swore softly. "I did go to the local

library to see if I could find anything on the mine that I don't already have."

"Were you online? Or does the library even have computers? I haven't been there."

"Actually, they do have computers, but I was in the local-history section—oh my God!"

"What? You remembered something!"

"I had my stuff on one of the tables and turned my back on it for about five minutes while I searched the stacks for an old Spanish history book that your great-great-grandfather originally gave to the library."

"And that was just enough time for someone to lift your room key."

"But there was no one in the library but me and the librarian," she argued. "And she couldn't have been a day under seventy-five. I can't see her stealing my key, let alone ransacking my room."

She had a point, one he couldn't argue with. "Okay, so the odds are she didn't do it, but just because you didn't see anyone doesn't mean that there wasn't anyone there. If you were really concentrating on the book you were looking for, you probably wouldn't have heard a freight train if it had roared past."

"I wouldn't say that," she said with a quick frown, "but yes, I do tend to get caught up in my research sometimes and lose track of what's going on around me. But surely I would have noticed if someone was scrounging around in my purse. And how would they have even known I was at the library…unless they were following me?"

He watched her pale and couldn't blame her for not liking the direction of her thoughts. He didn't like them, either, but they had to consider the possibility. "I think you should move out to the ranch for the rest of your stay," he said. "Just as a precaution. You're not safe here by yourself."

Her stomach in knots at the idea of staying in her motel room after a stranger had put his hands all over her things, she wanted to jump at his offer and grab on to it with both hands. But she was and always would be a woman alone—she'd decided that the day she divorced Carl—and Buck Wyatt was only in her life for a temporary time. She had to solve her own problems or live with them.

"I'll be fine," she assured him with a smile that didn't come nearly as easily as she'd have liked. "I'm sure the police will make more rounds by the motel, but even if they don't, I shouldn't have any more problems. Whoever searched my room likely won't be back. What would be the point? They've already seen everything I have."

"No, they've seen what you left in your room," he argued. "If they've got any brains at all, they know that you probably took what they're looking for with you. Which means, unfortunately, that they'll be back. I'm not trying to scare you, love, but next time, they'll come looking for you."

She'd already come to that same conclusion, and she didn't mind admitting that it scared the socks off of her. But she couldn't let Buck see that, couldn't let him know how much she wanted to walk into his arms and let him protect her. They only had two weeks together— *two weeks!*—and she couldn't let herself make the mistake of thinking he was her knight in shining armor. They were just business partners. Why did she have such a difficult time remembering that?

"I'll be fine," she insisted. "I'll call the desk and move to a room on the front side of the motel. The next time anyone decides to break in and go through my things, they'll have to do it in full view of anyone who happens to be driving past."

Frustrated, Buck just wanted to shake her. "You have got to be the most stubborn woman I've ever met in my life! Don't you get it? You could be in real danger, Rainey. You don't need notes to find the treasure. Oh, you've got a map, such as it is, but that's not going to mean anything to anyone but you. All you really need is what's in your head! And whoever trashed your room knows that. Next time they come back, they could be coming back for you."

"Then they'll find themselves talking to the wrong end of my pistol," she retorted. "I sleep with it next to my bed every night."

"And if whoever breaks in is some bad-ass dude, as you Americans put it. Someone who could take it away from you before you could even blink? Then what?"

"Then I'll…deal with it. And don't ask me how," she added quickly, scowling at him. "I don't know. Okay? I'll just deal with it when it happens."

He'd never met a more frustrating woman in his life. He didn't care how long she'd been treasure hunting or how experienced she was. She couldn't weigh more than a hundred and twenty pounds dripping wet. Any man with an ounce of testosterone in his veins could push her around with one hand tied behind his back.

But he only had to look at the stubborn set of her chin to know that she was in no mood to hear that or anything else. She'd made up her mind that she could take care of herself. He could talk until he was blue in the face, and he wasn't going to get anywhere.

"Obviously, I can't hog-tie you and force you to stay at the ranch," he said flatly. "It's your call. If you change your mind, you know where I live."

"I won't," she said, "but thanks for the offer. And thanks for coming to my rescue. I didn't even think when I realized the door to my room was open—I just grabbed my phone and called you. I didn't really expect you to drive all the way into town, but it was very sweet of you. Thank you."

Surprising him, she stepped forward to press a quick kiss to his cheek. Her eyes met his, and suddenly, he couldn't forget the long, hot kiss they'd shared earlier. Heat sparked like the flame of a match, and without even realizing how it happened, they were whisper close.

Alarm bells clanging in his head, Buck couldn't take his eyes off her mouth. All too easily, he could remember the heat and taste of her, and it was driving him crazy. One more kiss wouldn't hurt anything—

"I have to go," she said huskily. "Don't forget to call me when the Jeep's ready so we can start the search."

She stepped back before he could stop her, and he was left with no choice but to do the same thing. "If that's the way you want it," he said grimly. "Go inside and lock the door. I'm not leaving until I know you're safe."

"I'll be fine—"

"Go inside, Rainey."

She went, though reluctantly. Only when he heard her turn the dead bolt did he climb back into the pickup and head home.

Leaning back against the closed door, Rainey listened to the sound of the pickup as it disappeared in the distance and fought the need to call Buck back. This was, she knew, for the best. So why did she feel so incredibly lonely?

Shaking off the feeling, she reached for the phone and called the front desk to request a room change. Then she packed.

Hours later, in the dark silence of the night, Main Street was a ghost town. A lone cat darted through the shadows, chasing a late dinner, while the wind pushed an empty Coke can down the street, sending it clattering into the curb.

Alone in her new motel room, Rainey never noticed. Slipping deeper into sleep, into her waiting dreams, she sighed as images of Buck pulled at her, teased her, stirred fantasies she wouldn't allow to surface in the light of day. With a murmur that was his name, she turned in to her pillow, reaching for him, aching.

The phone rang suddenly, like a scream in the night. Startled, Rainey jerked awake, her heart thundering like a runaway train. "What…?"

Confused, she thought her alarm was going off, only to realize it was the phone. Blindly, she reached for it in the dark. "'Lo?"

"Stay away from Buck Wyatt," a cold male voice growled in her ear. "If you help him find the mine, you'll live to regret it."

Chapter 6

Dressed in her nightgown and robe, Rainey stood in the open doorway of her motel room and scowled at Officer Tucker like he'd just crawled out from under a rock. "What do you mean…*you can't do anything?* Somebody just called and threatened me!"

"I'm well aware of that, Ms. Brewster, but—"

"But nothing! First you can't do anything about someone breaking into my room and now you don't care that someone's threatening me? I thought the police were supposed to protect people! What kind of place is this?"

"We are here to protect you," he said patiently.

"Then do something! Trace the call, for God's sake! It came through the motel switchboard, didn't it? Talk to someone in the office. There must be a record."

"It's not that simple," he replied. "The call was dialed directly to your room, so we're going to have to get phone records from the phone company, find out how many calls—if any—were made to the hotel at the time yours came in, then track down the different callers and identify them. That takes time, and I can't even get started until morning. So there's not much I can do right now except advise you to keep your door dead bolted. If you have any more problems, don't hesitate to call."

Yeah, right, Rainey thought. What good would it do to call if the police weren't going to do anything? "I'll be sure to do that," she said dryly. "And you'll let me know what you find out from the phone company."

"Of course," he assured her. "In the meantime, have a nice night."

If she hadn't been so upset, Rainey would have laughed. *A nice night?* Oh, sure. She didn't doubt for a minute that she'd sleep like a baby.

Shutting her door, she shot the dead bolt, only to shiver as her eyes fell on the silent telephone. Whoever called and threatened her had dialed her room direct. And that meant only one thing—he'd been out there somewhere in the dark, watching her, as she moved to her new motel room. Just the thought of that—and his threats—turned her blood to ice. Was he still watching her room, waiting for her to fall asleep again so he could kick her door in and catch her off guard?

Restless, furious with herself for feeling scared, she told herself she was being an idiot. Anyone who would call a woman in the middle of the night and threaten her was nothing but a coward. He was just pushing her buttons, and she was letting him. If she was smart, she'd unplug the damn phone and go back to bed.

But even as she reached for the light switch, she knew she couldn't do it. Inside, she was shaking. She wouldn't sleep the rest of the night.

Obviously, I can't hog-tie you and force you to stay at the ranch. It's your call. If you change your mind, you know where I live.

Buck's words whispered in her ear, reminding her that she didn't have to be alone. The choice was hers.

No! she told herself firmly. She wasn't running to Buck for help. This was her problem—she could handle it. But even as she tried to assure herself that all she had to do was keep the dead bolt locked, she knew it wasn't that simple. She could handle danger when she knew where it was coming from, but this was different. This was a nameless, faceless man who, apparently, used the darkness of the night as cover and watched her every move. Just thinking about the cold, deadly warning of his phone call still had the power to chill her to the bone. She didn't doubt for a minute that he would hurt her if she helped Buck find the mine.

Shivering at the thought, she hugged herself. She didn't care what Officer Tucker said—the door could have a hundred dead bolts, and she still wasn't going to feel safe.

She had to get out of there.

Her heart pounding, she whirled and grabbed her

suitcase. Seconds later, she was throwing everything she owned into it. Within minutes, the room was stripped bare of all her possessions.

It wasn't until she was at the door and reaching for the dead bolt, however, that she realized going to the ranch wasn't as simple as walking out the door and checking out of the motel. Because there was a very good possibility that the man who had called and threatened her was still out there in the dark, watching her room, waiting for her to do something stupid.

Blanching at the thought, she froze, her fingers trembling as they closed around the lock. What were the chances he was still out there? she wondered, shaken. Maybe she should call Officer Tucker and ask him to escort her to the Broken Arrow—

No! she thought, stiffening. If Tucker followed her out to the ranch, he would probably have to include it in some kind of report, and before she knew it, the entire town—and the sicko who was threatening her—would know where she was. She had to find another way.

She would, she decided, wait him out. It was nearly one-thirty in the morning. If she turned out the lights and pretended to go back to bed, maybe he would give up on the idea of watching her and return to whatever hole he'd slithered out of. Then, when it was safe, she would slip out under the cover of darkness and head for the ranch.

She didn't even try to sleep. Instead, she sat in the chair at the desk and stared at the clock in the dark. One hour stretched into another, and it was the longest two hours of her life. In the silence of the night, all she could hear was the frantic slamming of her heart against her ribs.

When she finally rose to her feet and soundlessly approached the door, her palms were damp and her legs anything but steady. Still, she didn't hesitate as she slung the strap of her laptop over her shoulder, grabbed her suitcase and quietly opened the door.

Outside, the wind had picked up and turned cold. Shivering, Rainey sank back against the door to her room and searched the darkness for signs of an unwanted watcher in the night. Nothing moved but the trees that swayed in the wind. Still wary, she judged the distance to her car. It was only five or six feet to the driver's door, but it seemed like miles. Dragging in a quick breath, she hit the unlock button of her keyless entry and ran for the car.

Long minutes after she threw her luggage in the back and herself in the driver's seat, her heart was racing like a runaway train, but there was no time to catch her breath. With a quick flick of her wrist, she started the car, backed out of the parking space, then hit the accelerator and raced out of the lot.

Main Street was, not surprisingly, deserted. It was nearly four in the morning, and most residents were at home in their beds. The truck stop at the far end of the street was open twenty-four hours a day, and there was a black sedan at the pumps, but there was no sign of the driver.

Relieved, she turned in the opposite direction and tried not to floorboard the accelerator as she headed out of town. To reach the Broken Arrow, she should have turned right instead of left, but just in case someone was still watching her, she wanted him to think she was leaving town. So she turned left and raced into the darkness just beyond the edge of town. Now all she had to do was find a road that would circle back and take her to the Broken Arrow.

His head buried under his pillow, Buck normally slept like the dead. But he hadn't been able to get Rainey out of his head from the moment he'd lain down, and his sleep was anything but peaceful. A man in a black mask haunted his dreams, chasing Rainey in the night, and all he could hear were her cries. Disturbed, he tossed and turned and hovered on the edge of consciousness for what seemed like hours.

When an unexpected ringing seemed to float through the house, echoing Rainey's cries for help, he frowned and buried his head deeper into his pillow. Then it dawned on him what the sound was…the doorbell.

Startled, he came awake abruptly, his eyes immediately flying to the clock on his nightstand: 4:00 a.m.! What the hell? Who the devil was ringing his doorbell at that hour of the morning? Scowling in the darkness, he threw off the covers and reached for his jeans.

The last person he expected to see on his doorstep in the middle of the night was Rainey. Jerking the door all the way open, he pulled her inside. "What's wrong? What are you doing here? Are you all right?"

"Yes…well, sort of—"

"What do you mean…*sort of?* You either are or you're not. What happened?"

Shivering, she hugged herself. "I got a phone call."

"From whom?"

"Some jerk," she retorted. "He threatened me, said I'd regret it if I helped you find the mine."

Scowling again, he swore roundly. "When was this? Dammit, Rainey, you should have called me! Did you get in touch with Tucker?"

She nodded grimly. "Not that it did much good. He claimed there wasn't a lot he could do. Whoever threatened me, phoned my room directly, so the motel doesn't have a record of the call. He'll have to trace it through the phone company."

"And when was this?"

"A couple of hours ago," she admitted.

"A *couple of hours!*" he sputtered. "And you're just now getting here? What have you been doing? Wait a minute," he said before she could answer. "You changed rooms after I left, didn't you? The only way that jackass could have known your room number was if he was watching you. Bloody hell! You must have been scared out of your mind!"

"That's why it took me so long to get here," she admitted huskily. "I was afraid he was hiding in the dark, watching me, so I turned out the lights and pretended to go back to bed. After a couple of hours, I figured he probably got tired of waiting. So I threw everything in my car and came out here. I hope you don't mind. You did offer."

"Of course I don't mind," he retorted. "You'll be safer here—no one's going to know where you are except me and David, and he's not telling anyone. Did anyone follow you?"

"No," she sighed, relieved. "I only saw two cars, and one was a deputy sheriff making his rounds."

"Good. But you should have called me," he scolded her as he took her suitcase and computer from her. "You didn't have to go through that alone."

How could she tell him that she was afraid to become too dependent on him? That he was too easy to lean on? Too easy to trust? To care about—

Stiffening at the thought, she said quickly, "I couldn't do that to you a second time. Instead, I show up on your doorstep at four o'clock in the morning."

"Do you hear me complaining? Come on. I'll take you to your room," he said with a wry smile.

He started up the stairs, but she never budged from where she stood in the foyer. Surprised, he stopped four steps up and frowned over his shoulder at her. "Are you coming?"

She hesitated. "Do you have a guesthouse? Maybe I should stay there."

"You could," he agreed. "The guesthouse is about a hundred yards from the main house. It's quiet—and deserted. You're welcome to stay there, of course, but you'll be out of sight of the house."

She paled at the thought. She wouldn't sleep a wink.

"I really think you'd feel safer in the main house," he told her sincerely. "I'll be right down the hall, and the house has a security system. The guesthouse doesn't."

Put that way, there was no decision to make. "You're right. I'll feel safer in the guestroom."

"Good. There are clean towels in the bathroom and fresh sheets on the bed," he said as he started up the stairs again. "And feel free to make yourself at home in the kitchen if you're hungry."

"Actually, I just want to go to bed and get some sleep," she said honestly. "I'm exhausted."

"I'm not surprised," he said as they reached the top of the stairs and he pushed open the door to the first door on the left. "Sleep as late as you like in the morning," he told her. "David and I have to take care of the Jeep, so you might as well catch up on your sleep. Later, we'll figure out what we're going to do about the search for the mine."

A half smile curled the corners of her mouth. "I should warn you that I feel like I could sleep around the clock. I hope that's not a problem."

"Not at all," he assured her. "If you don't mind, though, I'd like to put your car in the garage. If no one knows you're here, we want to keep it that way."

"Oh my God, I didn't even think of that!" Quickly digging her keys out of her purse, she handed them over. "Hopefully, the jackass who threatened me will think he scared me into leaving town."

"The man's a coward," he said flatly. "Even if he suspects you didn't leave town, you don't have to worry. He's not going to get to you here. Not only will I call the cops if he even thinks about showing up here, I won't hesitate to shoot his ass if he dares to try to step foot on the property."

Buck might have been British right down to the tips of his toes, but there was no question that his Wyatt roots ran deep. When it came to a fight, Rainey didn't doubt for a minute that he was a man who came out on top. She just hoped it didn't come to that.

"Whoever he is, I don't think he'll have the guts to show up here," she said quietly. "Or at least not openly. He's too much of a coward for that."

"He won't if he's got any brains," he retorted grimly. "So go to bed and don't worry about anything. Everything's fine."

When he wished her a husky good-night and shut the door behind him, she almost called him back. She knew she was safe, knew he would do whatever he had to to protect her. But in the silence that enveloped her with his leave-taking, an unfamiliar loneliness pulled at her, surprising her.

What was going on? she wondered, frowning in the darkness as she changed into her pajamas for the second time that night and crawled into bed. She'd never been one of those women who needed other people to distract her from the loneliness of her own existence. Her job was a solitary one, but she was content with her own company. And when she needed companionship, she had no trouble finding someone to laugh and talk and share a meal with. So why, all of a sudden, did she feel so miserable? What was wrong with her?

"You're just tired," she said out loud, breaking the silence that was as dark as the night. "You'll feel better in the morning."

Closing her eyes, she willed herself to sleep. She might as well have demanded that her black hair turn blond overnight. It wasn't going to happen. She found herself listening to the sounds of the house, to Buck as he came back inside after moving her car to the garage. A door shut downstairs, then his firm sure footsteps echoed in the stillness of the night as he reached the top of the stairs and strode past her bedroom. A few seconds later, a door shut farther down the hall, and once again, the night turned quiet.

How long she lay there, trying to still the thoughts jumping around in her head, she couldn't have said. It could have been minutes, hours. Then her stomach started grumbling.

Feel free to make yourself at home in the kitchen if you're hungry.

Her stomach grumbled again as Buck's words echoed in her ears. No! she told herself fiercely. She wasn't going to go rumbling around in his kitchen in the middle of the night. She just needed to go to sleep.

But it had been a long time since supper—she couldn't even remember if she'd eaten—and she was starving. If she could just have a piece of toast or something, she was sure she'd sleep like a baby. It wouldn't take ten minutes.

The decision made, her mouth already watering, she threw off the covers and felt around in the dark with her feet for her house shoes. Five seconds later, she quietly opened her bedroom door. In the hall, strategically placed night-lights led the way to the stairs. Her house shoes whispering across the carpet, she headed downstairs to the kitchen.

Buck liked to think he was a gentleman. He wouldn't take advantage of a woman, especially when she was sleeping under his roof. But oh, he wanted to. He wanted to feel Rainey turn soft and hot when he kissed her....

Swearing at the direction of his thoughts, he punched his pillow into a more comfortable position, but it didn't help. Nothing helped because he couldn't forget that she was sleeping just down the hall. He was, he thought in disgust, losing his mind.

Deciding he wasn't going to get any sleep unless he took a cold shower, he rolled out of bed and headed for the bathroom. He'd only taken three steps, however, when he heard a sound downstairs.

What the hell? Freezing, he cocked his head, listening, and tried to convince himself he was just imagining things. Rainey was safely in her room, and the house was locked up tight. His ears were playing tricks on him.

Downstairs, a door quietly shut.

So much for imagination, he thought grimly, and reached for his jeans. Imagination didn't open and close doors.

As silent as a panther tracking a rabbit, he slipped out of his room and soundlessly ran down the stairs in his bare feet. At the foot of the stairs, he stopped, listening. From the kitchen, something fell, something that sounded like a cooking utensil.

A knife? he thought with a scowl, swearing silently. How the devil had the jackass gotten in to begin with? And what did he plan to do with a knife? Slit their throats? Bloody hell!

Standing in the dark in the entry hall, he glanced around, searching the deep shadows for something to protect himself with. Then he remembered the umbrella in the stand right next to the front door. As far as weapons went, an umbrella hardly qualified, but he did have the element of surprise on his side. If nothing else, he could disarm the intruder before the bloke even knew anyone in the house was awake.

Soundlessly stepping over to the umbrella stand, he grabbed an umbrella and quietly pulled it out. Almost immediately, the others shifted into the vacated space. They only made a faint whisper of sound, but in the stillness of the night, the sigh of material rubbing against material ripped through the silence like a scream. Swallowing a curse, he froze.

Later, he couldn't have said how long he stood there

in the darkness, waiting for the intruder to come racing out of the kitchen with a knife. But whoever was in there seemed to be searching the place. Cabinet doors were opened, then shut, and he thought he heard a curse. What the hell was the bastard looking for?

Gripping the umbrella like it was a club, he silently approached the kitchen's closed swinging door. There was no window in it, so he couldn't see who was on the other side—and he was going to change that the first chance he got, he promised himself. For now, he could only hope the bastard didn't have a gun.

Braced for a fight, his heart pounding, he dragged in a calming breath, silently counted to three, then kicked the door in. "Freeze, you son of a bitch!"

Startled, Rainey screamed and dropped the jar of grape jelly she was holding. It hit the floor with a crash and shattered. Her eyes wide in her pale face, she didn't even notice. "Buck! What...!"

"What the hell!" Shocked, he suddenly realized he was holding the umbrella like he was going to knock her head off. Muttering a curse, he dropped it with a clatter. "What are you doing down here? I heard a noise and thought it was a burglar."

"I'm sorry. I was hungry. You said I could use the kitchen, so I was going to make a peanut butter and jelly sandwich." Her eyes dropping to his bare feet, which were just inches from the broken jelly jar, she gasped, "Don't move! Where's the broom?"

"I have no idea," he said honestly. "Here…let me do that. It was my fault. I scared you."

"No. I can do it. You'll cut yourself."

They both moved at the same time, stooping down to clean up the spilled jelly and broken glass, and suddenly found themselves so close they were practically knee to knee.

Startled, Rainey's eyes met his and in the time it took to blink, she couldn't seem to breathe. And it was all Buck's fault. "I'm the one who dropped it," she said. "I should be the one to clean it up."

"You wouldn't have dropped it if I hadn't scared you to death," he pointed out in a voice as rough as sandpaper. "Anyway, you're a guest—"

"A messy guest," she retorted, smiling. "And I thought I was being so quiet. How did you hear me?"

"I've always been a light sleeper," he admitted. "Especially when someone else is in the house. I thought I heard something downstairs, then a door shut. Just as I came down the stairs, it sounded like you dropped a knife or something."

"I did," she admitted. "A butter knife for the peanut butter and jelly."

He grinned. "I had an image in my head of this great big burly bloke grabbing a butcher knife and coming upstairs to kill you."

"So you grabbed an umbrella?"

"It was the only thing close at hand," he laughed. "I was hoping to have the element of surprise on my side."

"Oh, you surprised me, all right," she chuckled. "I'll never be able to eat peanut butter and jelly again without thinking about umbrellas."

"And me."

Her heart thumping at his words, she couldn't deny it. Peanut butter and jelly and umbrellas aside, he was, she knew, going to be hard to forget. "And you," she agreed, only to wince at the revealing huskiness of her voice. Flustered, she quickly returned her attention to the mess on the floor. "We've got to get this cleaned up. Let me get some paper towels."

Rising quickly to her feet, she stepped over to the counter and grabbed a roll of paper towels from the holder next to the sink. Pulling a handful off the roll, she handed them to Buck, then rolled off the same for herself. Once again practically knee to knee with him, she began to carefully clean up the jelly and broken glass.

Long seconds later, the floor was clean, but she couldn't be sure that they'd gotten every sliver of glass. "You know, you really shouldn't walk around barefoot until the floor has had a good sweeping. Let me look for the broom."

"No." Grabbing her hand before she could turn away, he said gruffly, "I'll do that later. I'm going back to bed, anyway. What about you? Are you still hungry?"

He still held her hand, making it impossible for her to think about anything except the heat of his touch. Her blood starting to hum, she could only shake her head. "No, I don't think so."

"You sure? There's more jelly in the pantry."

His thumb rubbed the back of her hand, making her weak at the knees. Her fingers curled around his. What had he asked? Suddenly remembering, she frowned. "No…thank you. I'm not really hungry anymore."

"Then let's go to bed."

"Buck!"

"I didn't mean together. Oh! Is that what you were thinking?" he teased. "Why didn't you say so, love? Let's go!"

"No!" she laughed. "I didn't mean—"

"Are you sure? Maybe I can change your mind."

Unable to stop grinning, she tugged at her hand. "Oh no you don't, mister. Behave yourself."

"Make me," he taunted, and pulled her into his arms.

Her heart already thundering with expectation, she went willingly and told herself she wasn't going to lose her head over one little kiss. Then he pulled her close against him and his mouth closed over hers and the teasing kiss she expected turned into something dark and hot and tempting. With a nearly silent moan, she lost herself in the taste and feel and heat of him.

When they both finally came up for air, she could hardly remember her own name. When she realized she didn't care, she knew she was in trouble. Dear God, what had he done to her?

His eyes dark with need, he started to kiss her again, but she moved, lightning quick. "I'm going to bed," she said breathlessly. "Alone!"

He didn't, thankfully, come after her. Instead, he waited until she was almost to the door before he called out, "Sure I can't change your mind?"

"Good night, Buck," she said firmly. "I'll see you in the morning."

Color burning her cheeks, she hurried upstairs to her room, but long after Buck went to his own room and she crawled back into bed, she couldn't forget how she'd lost herself in his kiss. Every time he kissed her, she found it harder and harder to step out of his arms. And for no other reason than that, she should have jumped in her car and gotten out of there. It would have been the smart thing to do.

So why was she still there?

She tried to tell herself that it was because of the mine. She'd been reading about it, researching it, dreaming about finding it, for as long as she could remember. Now that she had a legitimate chance of finding it, she couldn't just walk away. Not when it could be the biggest find of her career. Buck or no Buck, she was going to stick it out.

For her own peace of mind, though, she prayed they found the mine quickly. Because if she let Buck kiss her again the way he had tonight, she was going to be in serious trouble.

Chapter 7

Five days later, Buck stood beside the Jeep, which *finally* had new brakes, and swore in disgust as he surveyed the entrance to one of the Broken Arrow's largest canyons. "Do you realize how many canyons we've looked at this week?" he asked Rainey.

"Twelve," she said promptly. "And they all look alike."

He couldn't argue with that. "I don't know how the devil the Spaniards found their way back to the mine whenever they left to go to the mission for supplies or church or just contact with the outside world. I know they planted a tree and it was the only one for miles, but how did they even find that? The canyons stretch all the way to the horizon. How did they keep from getting lost?"

"They would have kept the mine's location a secret,"

she pointed out, "so they wouldn't have left any markers to point the way."

"No, but they would have made a map with coordinates," he said. "In your research, you never came across anything like that?"

"No." She sighed. "But that's not surprising. It's been over two hundred years since the Spanish discovered the mine. There's no telling what happened to the map."

Frowning at a sudden thought, he shot her a sharp look. "But what if the map wasn't destroyed and someone found it? How do you know they didn't find the mine and strip it of its ore a hundred years ago?"

"If the Spanish had found it and started working it again, there would have definitely been a record of it in Spain."

He scowled at the horizon, at the canyons that blended one into the other toward the mountains in the distance. "So we have to assume the mine's out there somewhere. And we're not any closer to finding it than we were at the beginning of the week."

"It's been lost for centuries," Rainey replied. "We knew this wasn't going to be easy."

"We've got to find another way," he told her. "We're spending hours every day driving out to the canyons, then going back to the house at night. We need to just stay out here."

"We could camp out," she suggested. "The weather's been great."

"I have a better idea," he retorted. "David has a

camper. It's got a heater and stove, a bathroom, everything. We'll use that."

"He won't mind?"

"No. He told me when I hired him that I could use it whenever I liked. I could call him when we get back to the house, but I hate to bother him. His mom is terminally ill. He's got enough on his plate without worrying about what's going on back here."

"Have you heard from him?"

He nodded. "Hospice has been called in. The doctors don't expect her to last past the end of the week."

"And David has no brothers or sisters? He's going through this all alone? That's really sad."

"He seems to be holding up pretty well," he said gruffly. "Of course, he has to. There is no one else."

"If you're sure he won't mind if we use the camper, that really would save us a lot of travel time."

"Good. Then we'll go back to the house and get everything together. We're going to need food, clothes, sleeping bags. How long will it take you to get ready?"

Rainey hardly heard him. *Sleeping bags?* What kind of camper was he talking about? He'd said it had a bathroom and stove, but what if it was just a shell that closed in the pickup bed and mattress on a platform? They would be sleeping side by side in what was little more than a tin can—

"Rainey? Was it something I said? Where'd I lose you?"

She blinked…and glanced up to find him watching her with wicked amusement. The second her eyes met his, she knew he'd guessed exactly what she was thinking. Darn the man! How did he do this to her? She'd never been shy with a man before, let alone blushed like a sixteen-year-old virgin! What was wrong with her?

Not even daring to try to answer that question, she cursed the hot color stinging her cheeks and met his gaze with an arch look that didn't come as easily as she would have liked. "I beg your pardon?"

"You seem to have a problem with the camper," he retorted. "Or did I misunderstand?"

"I've been camping since I was an infant," she informed him loftily. "I don't have a problem with campers or with roughing it, for that matter."

"Good. So how long will it take you to pack?"

"I can be ready to leave whenever you are."

He grinned. "Really? It's one-thirty now. It'll be two-thirty by the time we get back to the house. I'll meet you at the front door at three-thirty. With both of us loading, we should be able to leave by four, at the latest."

"Isn't that kind of late to get started?" she said with a frown. "You know what happened the last time we did that."

He grinned. "We won't have to walk back to the homestead—I promise. It just seems more practical to leave this afternoon. Then we'll reach the canyons before dark, and we can start the search again at first light. But if you want to wait until tomorrow so you can wash your hair and take a bath and sleep in a real bed one more time, then we can wait until morning. It's your call."

She should have told him that was exactly what she wanted to do, but not because she wanted to put off roughing it one more day. She needed space—from him—but nothing short of Chinese water torture was going to make her admit that. Lifting her chin, she said coolly, "I'll be out front at three-thirty. If you're late, you cook dinner."

Grinning, he held out his hand to shake on the deal. "And if you are, you do…and the dishes."

"Did I mention that I like to come in first?"

Delighted, he laughed as she placed her hand in his and gave him a firm shake. "So do I," he said. "Looks like one of us is going to lose. It's not going to be me."

Far from troubled, she only smiled. "We'll see. Oh, just for the record, I like my steak medium well done. I don't want it to moo."

"Have it any way you like, love. You're cooking it."

The line was drawn in the sand, and Rainey couldn't have been more pleased. As long as she focused on the competition between them, she could forget the hot, intoxicating fire of his kiss…until he kissed her again. And he would kiss her again. She only had to look in his eyes to know that it would be soon.

The second they reached the house, Rainey jumped out of the Jeep before it rolled to a complete stop. "Don't forget the sour cream for my baked potato," she told him with a grin and ran upstairs for her things as soon as he unlocked the front door.

"Hey, the kitchen's the other way," he called after her. "You're going to need fajita seasoning for my steak. And I like steak fries. You do know how to peel a potato, don't you?"

Her only response was a giggle.

Watching her disappear upstairs, Buck wondered if she had any idea how irresistible she was. Later, that was going to bother him, but he didn't have time to worry about that now. He not only had to get his own things, but food and sleeping bags for the two of them and move the camper to the front driveway. And the clock was ticking.

He sprinted up the stairs. He hoped like hell Ms. Indiana Jones knew how to cook. He hated to see a good steak ruined.

The next hour passed in a flash. Anticipating the look on Rainey's face when she stepped out the front door and found him waiting for her, he threw his clothes in the camper, moved David's pickup and camper to the circular driveway in front of the house, then hurried into the kitchen to collect enough food for their stay in the wilderness. One of the first things he'd done when he moved to the ranch was stock the freezer and pantry in case he got snowed in, so he was ready for just about anything. Grinning as he grabbed steaks and chops and bacon from the freezer, he reminded himself to get fajita seasoning from the pantry. He'd never tasted the stuff before he'd moved to the States, and now he was addicted to it.

He hoped Rainey liked it, because she was going to be cooking with it a lot. If he planned his bets right, she'd end up cooking every meal. And nothing tasted better than someone else's cooking. Damn, he was going to enjoy this.

His eyes dancing with anticipation, he hurriedly collected the last few items they would need and strode out the front door. By the time Rainey got her things together and came downstairs, he'd have everything put up and be stretched out in the overhead cab, taking a nap.

He could already taste the steak.

He liked to think he wasn't a man who gloated, but as he pulled open the rear door to the camper, he was humming. Then he saw Rainey. *She* was lying in the bed over the cab, watching him with a grin that was quick and cocky and triumphant.

Stunned, he nearly dropped the bags of groceries he was holding. "What the hell! You couldn't have packed already!"

"Actually, I never unpacked," she said with a chuckle. "All I had to do was zip my case and grab my pillow. I've been waiting on you for the last fifteen minutes. What took you so long?"

Buck had to laugh. She'd set him up and he'd never seen it coming. "Why do I feel like I've been had?"

"Because you have. Did I happen to mention that I'm really looking forward to supper?"

He just gave her a baleful look. "You're going to gloat, aren't you?"

"Yeah, I am."

"Go ahead," he growled. "Enjoy yourself. Just remember…what goes around, comes around. And I don't lose very often. Your day's coming."

"Promises, promises," she retorted with dancing eyes. "I'm shaking in my shoes."

"Keep it up," he warned. "I'm taking notes."

"Okay," she laughed, giving in. "I'll behave…later! I'm hungry. How about you? When's supper?"

She was outrageous—and thoroughly enjoying herself. If Buck thought she would show a little restraint when they climbed into the cab of the truck and headed down the driveway, he soon found out that Rainey didn't know the meaning of the word *restraint*. Sitting beside him, she chatted happily…about supper. He wanted to shoot her—but he couldn't stop laughing.

"And tomorrow night, when you lose the next bet—" Suddenly distracted when he turned away from the ranch road they usually took to the canyons, she sat up straighter, frowning. "Hey, where are we going? I thought we were camping in the canyons so we wouldn't have to come back to the house every night."

"We are," he assured her. "But there's a back entrance to the ranch through the national forest. It's never used—it's padlocked, in fact, and I'm the only one with a key. We'll drive up there, go as far as we can in the truck, then go the rest of the way on foot."

"And if we don't find the right canyon?"

"Then we'll hike back to the truck and drive deeper

into the mountains." Taking his eyes from the road only long enough to send her an arch look, he said, "Any more objections?"

Her blue eyes sparkled with excitement. "You can't get there fast enough for me. Let's go."

Reaching the end of the driveway, he turned onto the winding, two-lane road that bordered the Broken Arrow to the north. There wasn't another vehicle in sight. Pastureland quickly gave way to the national forest, and soon they were climbing in elevation as the road twisted and turned and went every which way but straight.

"God, it's beautiful up here," Rainey said as the trees on their left suddenly gave way to an open pasture where a herd of elk was grazing. "Do you hunt?"

"Only with a camera," he said, holding up the camera that she hadn't noticed in the console between them. "I take it with me wherever I go. I've gotten some pretty incredible shots of wildlife."

"I'll bet." Remembering a long-ago trip to Yellowstone, she smiled. "The first time I went to Yellowstone, I must have taken a picture of every deer and moose in sight. And that was before digital cameras! After I'd taken about fifteen rolls of film, my dad started making me pay for the development out of my savings."

"So how many more pictures did you take after that?"

"Oh, at least another ten rolls," she retorted. "We had pictures *everywhere!* Poor Daddy. He wanted to shoot me."

"Do you still have the pictures?"

She nodded. "I put them all in an album…well, make that four albums," she amended, "but who's counting?"

"I know how you feel," he said. "The first time I drove around the ranch and saw a bald eagle sitting in the top of a pine tree, surveying the river valley like he owned the place, I didn't have my camera with me. I've been taking it with me ever since."

"Have you seen a bear yet? I'll never forget the first time I saw one. I must have been around eight. We were staying up in the mountains at a friend's cabin north of Yellowstone, and I had just gone outside to play, when a bear stepped out from behind the garage. I was sure he was going to eat me. I started screaming for my dad and I was standing right by the door. He ribbed me about that for years."

She smiled just thinking about it, but she didn't think Buck had heard a word she said. His eyes kept shifting periodically to his side mirrors, and it was obvious that he didn't like whatever he saw there. Scowling, he muttered a very proper British curse and stepped on the accelerator, sending the truck surging forward.

Surprised, Rainey frowned. "What is it?" she began, only to gasp when she caught a glimpse of the huge black pickup truck in the passenger-side mirror. The trucker was right on their bumper. "Oh my God!"

"Yeah," he said grimly, keeping one eye on his mirror and the other on the road. "Someone's in a hell of a hurry."

"Is there somewhere we can pull over so he can get past us?"

Never taking his gaze from the curving road in front of him, Buck nodded. "If I remember correctly, there's a pullout just around the next curve. Our tailgater's not going to be happy about it, but I'm going to slow down. The camper's top heavy and a hell of a load—I'm not taking a chance on turning us over just because some jackass is late for a hot date."

He lifted his foot from the accelerator as he spoke and immediately dropped his speed. Behind him, the driver of the black pickup angrily laid on his horn and only crowded closer. "Dammit to hell!" Buck swore and raced into the pullout in a cloud of dust.

A split second later, the pickup raced past, its horn blaring as it missed their rear bumper by mere inches. Before Buck or Rainey could so much as gasp, the truck disappeared around the next curve.

Still swearing, Buck shot her a sharp look. "You all right?"

She laughed shakily. "That depends on how you look at it. I think I just lost ten years off my life. What about you?"

"I'm madder than hell," he retorted. "Other than that, I'm fine. Just peachy. Did you happen to get that jackass's license-plate number?"

"No. He went by too fast. I thought he had Colorado plates, but I couldn't swear to it."

He reached for his cell phone and checked to see if

he had service. "I've only got one bar, but I don't care. I'm going to see if I can reach the sheriff. He needs to get his butt out here and catch that jackass."

Before he could punch in 911, however, he looked up and swore. "Damnation!"

"What is it? Oh my God!"

Horrified, Rainey followed his gaze just in time to see the same black pickup that had practically run them off the road heading straight for them.

Locked in by her seat belt, Rainy couldn't do anything but sink back in her seat and watch in horror as the huge vehicle bore down on them at what seemed like the speed of sound. They were trapped—there was nowhere to go. To their right was nothing but a guard-rail…and the side of the mountain, which dropped away into nothingness. And to the left was the truck and the oncoming lane of traffic.

A wordless prayer rose to her lips. She was going to die. "Buck!"

"Hang on!" He hit the gas, and with a jerk of the wheel, sent them racing into the oncoming lane.

Rainey screamed—she must have. The sound of her own terror was still echoing in her ears when Buck hit the gas and jerked the wheel to the left again, sending them careening down an overgrown dirt road that was little more than a deer path through the trees. Buck never cut his speed. Then, just when Rainey was convinced the trees were going to rip the doors right off the truck, they skidded around a curve and Buck brought the vehicle to a shuddering stop.

The silence that enveloped them was sudden, complete, almost eerie. The thunder of her heart loud in her ears, Rainey just sat there, stunned. They weren't dead. She couldn't believe it.

"Are you all right?" Buck asked sharply.

"How in the world did you manage to get us through that in one piece?" she asked, wincing at the slight hysteria she heard in her voice. "I thought we were dead for sure."

"So did I," he admitted gruffly. "I had to do something or we were toast. I guess I'd better check and see what damage we did."

"I'll help," she said, pushing open her door. "I need to feel the ground under my feet."

Other than a few scratches, everything was fine. Looking at the top of the camper and the branches that clung to one of the vent pipes, she frowned. "Do you think we should check the roof?"

"Not now," he said. "We're almost to the ranch's back entrance, and I don't want to be trapped in these trees when that idiot comes looking for us."

Shocked, she said, "You think he'll come back a third time?"

"Don't you?"

Sick at the thought, she nodded miserably. "He must be crazy—"

"He may be crazy," he said coldly, "but he knew

exactly what he was doing. This was deliberate, Rainey. He was either trying to stop us from finding the mine or trying to put me in the hospital so I'd be away from the ranch for more than one night. Either way, we need to get out of here."

"Won't he be watching for us on the road?"

He smiled slightly. "This is our cutoff, Rainey. We won't be going back to the road. Or at least, we won't today."

"Thank God!" she sighed, only to frown as another thought hit her. "That's not going to stop him from looking for us. And if he catches us back here in these trees, we're going to be in big trouble."

"He went by us so fast that he didn't even see us turn off," he assured her as they both climbed back into the cab of the truck. "He probably thinks we're miles down the road by now. By the time he realizes we might have turned off, he won't have a clue where to start looking for us. There are cutoffs all through here—he'll have to search them all, and even if he comes down the right one, the gate will be locked, just as it always is, and there will be no sign that we were even here.

Rainey wanted to believe him, but she knew whoever had been driving the pickup was, in all likelihood, no fool. If he was determined to find them, he would.

"Everything's going to be fine, Rainey," he said quietly. "You could bring fifty men up here with bloodhounds and they wouldn't find us if we didn't want to be found."

The words were hardly out of his mouth when they reached the simple ranch gate that marked the back entrance to the Broken Arrow. Rainey took one look at it and immediately understood why Buck wasn't worried about being followed. The overgrown dirt road they'd taken from the main county road had narrowed to what was little more than a deer trail. Huge pines and firs stood shoulder to shoulder like ancient soldiers, cutting out what was left of the afternoon sun, creating deep, cold shadows and an early twilight. In the gathering darkness, a motorcycle would have had a difficult time winding its way through the trees—and they were in a pickup with a camper in the bed!

Shooting him a skeptical look, she lifted a delicately arched brow. "You can't be serious. We can't get through those trees."

"Oh, ye of little faith," he said as he pushed open his door and got out to unlock and open the gate. "It's not as bad as it looks."

Opening the gate wide, he pushed the truck's side mirrors flush against each door, then slid back into the driver's seat and carefully drove onto the ranch. Seconds later, after he'd closed and padlocked the gate again, he wound through the trees like a snake.

Holding her breath more than once, Rainey had to give him credit. He knew what he was doing. "I stand corrected," she told him when he reached a small clearing and turned to her with a triumphant grin. "You did that better than I could have, and you grew up driving with the steering wheel on the wrong side."

"How can it be on the wrong side when it's on the right side?" he quipped with twinkling eyes. "Do you really want to go there? You know that's an argument you're going to lose."

"I know nothing of the kind," she sniffed, fighting a smile and failing miserably. "Anyway, we don't have time to argue—it's going to be dark soon. Where are we going to make camp?"

"Let's play it by ear," he suggested. "We'll get as far as we can before dark."

The day was, in fact, fading fast. As they left the ranch entrance far behind and drove deeper into the wild territory that made up the northern section of the Broken Arrow, the shadows were soon all-enveloping. Then the terrain changed, and their progress slowed to a crawl. It wasn't until they came to an outcropping of huge rock boulders, however, that Buck stopped.

"Looks like this is the end of the road," he announced, cutting the engine. "In the morning, we might be able to find a way around these rocks, but for now, we'll stay here."

"Good," Rainey said as she peered out the windshield. "The wind's really picking up. Looks like a storm's brewing."

"The weatherman said we had a fifty-fifty chance of rain tonight. Too bad! There goes your steak."

"Oh, no!" she said quickly, grinning. "You're not

getting out of cooking that easily. You owe me a steak, mister. I'll let you off easy tonight, but tomorrow, you're grilling."

"Yes, ma'am. Whatever you say, ma'am. Now that we've got that settled, I suggest we both get into the camper before it starts pouring."

The words were hardly out of his mouth when lightning streaked across the night sky and thunder cracked directly overhead. Rainey jumped, startled and pushed open the passenger door to run for the camper. Buck had just joined her at the rear door when the skies opened up.

"Awhaaa! Hurry!"

"It's just rain," he teased. "You won't melt."

She narrowed her eyes at him. "You're going to melt if you don't hurry up and get this door open."

Laughing, he unlocked the door with a flick of the wrist and motioned her to precede him. "Ladies first."

The step up into the camper was high and slick. She needn't have worried. Before she could guess his intentions, Buck grabbed her around the waist from behind and lifted her into the camper. Gasping, she took two steps inside and stopped short. It was pitch-black inside—she couldn't see a thing.

Behind her, Buck stepped right into her and nearly knocked her flat on her face. Lightning quick, his arm snaked around her waist from behind, snatching her against him before she could fall. "Sorry, love," he growled in her ear. "It's a bit dark in here. Hold still and let me turn some lights on."

Chapter 8

His breath warm against the back of her neck, her heart pounding at the feel of him pressed close against her back, Rainey couldn't have moved if she'd wanted to. She told herself not to let her imagination run away with her—there was nothing the least bit romantic about his touch. He'd just caught her close instinctively to stop her from falling. Any man with any decency would have done the same.

Yeah, right, a voice in her head drawled. *So why are your senses humming if he's just doing the decent thing?*

She didn't have an answer for that, didn't even want to think of one. All she wanted to do was give in to the need to melt back against him. He was so close—she could feel every inch of him pressed against her, warming her all the way to her toes. And his voice. God, what his voice did to her! All she could think of was turning, crowding closer in the dark…

Just for a second, her body whispered in her ear. *What would it hurt?*

Even as she started to turn, to give in to the need that pulled at her, the voice of reason demanded to know what the devil she was doing. She didn't do this! She didn't go all googily-eyed over a man. Any man! Especially one who'd only recently broken up with his fiancée. And certainly not with one she was working with. That was the sure way to trouble. Their relationship had to be strictly business, nothing more.

So why did she have such a difficult time remembering that?

He moved to step around her, his body barely brushing hers in the dark, lingering just for a second, and in the time it took to draw in a quick, nearly soundless gasp, she couldn't seem to breathe. Her imagination stirred, teased, set her heart pounding. Then Buck flipped a switch and the camper was flooded with soft light.

"Better?" he asked.

She blinked, her heart still pounding, and couldn't manage a single word as she wrapped her arms around herself. Without his closeness, she was suddenly chilled.

"You need to get out of those damp clothes," he said gruffly as he turned on the light in the bathroom for her. "I'll wait outside while you change."

He was gone before she could argue, leaving behind

a silence she could hardly hear for the crazy beating of her heart. Grabbing her small suitcase from where she'd stored it in the closet earlier, she started to pull her pajamas from the case, only to hesitate. There was nothing the least bit revealing about her flannel pajamas and robe—she shouldn't have blinked twice at the thought of wearing them in front of Buck or anyone else. They were decent, and in another hour or two, it would be bedtime. She didn't want to change into dry clothes now, then into pajamas later. That was ridiculous. So why was she acting like a ninny?

Her chin set at a stubborn angle, she reached for her pajamas and robe and stepped into the bathroom.

The rain had eased, and the electrical storm had moved farther south, where lightning still danced an eerie dance in the night sky. Standing under the dripping trees, Buck drew in a rain-cooled breath, but it did little to ease the heat burning inside him. All he could think about was Rainey, slipping out of her wet clothes, her slender body damp and chilled....

Swearing at the direction of his thoughts, he focused instead on the weather. To the northwest, the sky was clearing, and one by one, the stars were coming out. It was going to be a cold night, but he doubted he'd notice...not when he would be practically sleeping with Rainey.

Oh, they weren't sharing a bed, he silently acknowledged, but they might as well have been. The camper was small, and Rainey was going to be sleeping all of three feet away from him. With no effort whatsoever, he could reach out and touch her.

Swearing softly at the thought, the memory of that moment when he'd caught her against him in the dark played in his head, teasing him, heating his blood, tempting him more than he'd ever thought possible. Whatever possessed him to agree to look for the mine with her? he wondered, irritated. He'd known he would be spending hours on end with her for days at a time, and the kisses they'd shared were right there between them every time their eyes met.

Not for the first time, he reminded himself she wasn't his type. It didn't seem to make a difference. He just had to look at her, to smell the damp, womanly scent of her, to imagine peeling her clothes from her with slow hands, and every nerve ending in his body focused completely on her. It was enough to push a sane man over the edge.

And it was going to stop, he told himself grimly. It had to. If he couldn't control himself, then maybe he needed to sleep in the cab of the truck. There was nothing like a little roughing it to bring a man to his senses.

For all of three seconds, he considered the idea, only to swear softly. What the devil was wrong with him? He'd never lost control with a woman in his life—he wasn't about to start now. All he had to do was keep his distance. Granted, the camper was small, but they were both adults and sleeping in separate beds. Keeping his hands to himself was *not* going to be a problem!

He gave her another five minutes, then knocked on the camper door. "Are you decent? I'm coming in."

"I was just trying to find a place to hang my damp things," she said as he stepped inside and shut the door behind him. "I found some hangers in the closet." Glancing around at her jeans and shirt spread out on hangers and hanging from overhead cabinets, she sent a quick look at a dark corner where her underwear was discreetly hanging.

"No problem," he assured her. He was thirty-two years old—he'd obviously seen women's underwear before. So why the devil did his eyes keep drifting toward the darkened corner where her panties hung? he thought with a silent groan. And how the heck could the woman look so incredible in flannel? It just wasn't fair!

"How about some dinner?" he said. "There's some sliced turkey in the refrigerator. How about a sandwich?"

"That's a long way from steak," she grumbled. Studying him consideringly, she said, "You know what that means, don't you? When you can't carry through on a bet?"

"No," he said dryly. "But let me guess. Now I owe you two dinners instead of one. Right?"

"Well, actually, I was thinking three, but I suppose I could agree to two dinners…and breakfast."

"Breakfast!"

"The easiest meal of the day," she assured him with twinkling eyes. "And you do owe me, you know. Of course, if you're the kind of man who welches on a bet—"

She was so outrageous, Buck had to laugh. "You're something else. You know that? Breakfast! All right. I give. I'll throw in breakfast, too. Happy now?"

"Well, you did say something about a turkey sandwich. I'll take mine with mayonnaise."

"Of course." He chuckled. "Anything else, Your Highness?"

"Soup," she said promptly.

"By all means," he agreed. "I'm one step ahead of you." And reaching into the cabinet, he pulled out a can of chicken noodle soup.

Dinner was hot, delicious and quick. By nine o'clock, the lights were turned out, the quiet of the night settled over them, and they were both in bed. Separate beds. Rainey should have fallen asleep the minute her head touched the pillow. She'd been up since before dawn and hadn't gone to bed until well after midnight for the last couple of nights. With no effort whatsoever, she shouldn't have been able to keep her eyes open. Instead, she lay there in the dark, her eyes searching the thick shadows for Buck.

Was he awake? she wondered, listening to him breathe. He had to be. He'd insisted that she take the bed over the cab of the truck, which was larger and more comfortable than where he'd settled in for the night— the tiny dinette, which converted into a sleeping berth when the table was taken down. A fifth-grader might have had plenty of room there, but Buck was six foot two, for heaven's sake! He crammed himself into the space like a sardine in a can and never uttered a single word of complaint.

Foolish man! Rainey thought, making no attempt to hold back a smile in the dark. She'd tried to tell him there was no need for him to be so chivalrous. She was eight inches shorter than he was, and this wasn't her first rodeo. Her job took her to out-of-the-way places all over the world, and nine times out of ten, there wasn't a motel anywhere in the vicinity. She'd learned a long time ago how to make herself comfortable in rough huts, caves, on the hard ground, even in trees, for heaven's sake! She could sleep in a dinette. Buck could not.

In the silence that enveloped the camper, she heard him shift in the dark, then swear under his breath. A giggle bubbled up in her throat. Before she could stop it, it escaped. Too late, she clamped a hand over her mouth, but she might as well have tried to hold back Niagara. Another laugh bubbled up, spilling onto the night air like an unexpected explosion of fireworks on a summer night, and that only made her want to laugh more.

"What, pray tell, is so bloody amusing?"

His indignant growl was all it took to push her over the edge. Burying her face in her pillow, she laughed until she cried.

Stuffed into the booth, Buck grinned in the darkness. So she thought this was funny, did she? Little witch. Her turn was coming. Tomorrow night, they would trade places.

"Go ahead and laugh," he told her, trying not to laugh himself. "You'll get yours."

"I'm shaking in my shoes, Prince Charming. In case you've forgotten, I offered to take the booth. You were the one who insisted on giving me the bigger bed."

"It was the gentlemanly thing to do," he retorted, only to swear as he cracked an ankle on the end of the booth when he tried to shift to a more comfortable position. "Don't you dare laugh."

She could just make him out in the darkness. He looked like a trussed turkey, with his knees up under his chin, and he still had to lie at an angle to even fit on the bed. "We can still switch, if you like," she offered. "Just say the word."

"No—"

"Buck, this is ridiculous. C'mon. Let's switch."

When he hesitated, she didn't give him time to argue. Throwing off her sleeping bag, she moved to the edge of the loftlike bed and fumbled for the small ladder that hooked onto the side.

"Wait! I'll turn on a light."

"That's okay. I don't need it," she assured him as she started down the ladder. "I—"

Without warning, her foot slipped on the metal ladder. Before she could do anything but gasp, she started to fall. *"What—"*

Crying out, she grabbed for purchase…and fell back

into Buck, whose bed was directly behind the ladder. Grunting, he caught her, only to lose his balance and fall backward onto his bed with her in his arms.

Later, Buck couldn't say how long they both lay there, stunned, gasping for breath in a tangle of arms and legs. It could have been seconds…hours. It didn't matter. Flannel pajamas had never felt so good on a woman.

With a will of their own, his hands slid over her back and hips even as he tried to convince himself that he was just checking to see if she was hurt. Unfortunately, he'd never lied worth a damn—especially to himself.

"Are you all right?" he rasped.

"I think so," she said, dazed, only to blink in horror when he suddenly switched on a light and she realized that not only was she sprawled on top of him, but their legs were intimately twined. Mortified, she felt her cheeks turn as red as her pajamas, but there wasn't a damn thing she could do about it except quip, "Well, isn't this awkward? Excuse me while I climb off you."

"Only if you insist," he retorted. "I don't mind. Really."

"You know, I had a feeling you'd say that," she said with a chuckle. "I'll pass, just the same." Her cheeks still burning, she quickly rolled off him and came to her feet in the narrow aisle next to the bed. Only then did the crazy pounding of her heart begin to ease.

Then she got a good look at him in his own pajamas and her mouth went dry. No man had a right to look so good in something as ordinary as pajamas. All he wore was the bottoms, which were blue-and-green plaid flannel, leaving his chest bare…and tantalizing. Why hadn't she realized there wasn't a spare ounce of fat on the man? He was lean and hard and fit, and all she wanted to do was run her hands over him.

Her eyes still focused on the hard muscles of his chest, she never saw his lips twitch. "Would you like me to put on my pajama shirt?" he asked, amused.

Startled, she blinked. "What? No! I mean yes!" Flustered, and more than a little irritated with herself, she wanted to sink right through the floor. She was stammering like a schoolgirl! All because the man stood before her without a shirt. What was wrong with her?

"It doesn't matter," she said stiffly, struggling to regain her dignity. "Wear whatever you want. I'm going to bed…as soon as you get out of it."

"Ah, yes, the bed," he said, and didn't budge. Instead, he studied her with twinkling eyes. Then he looked at the small bed. It was really only big enough for a twelve-year-old. "Are you sure you want to switch? I wouldn't put my worst enemy in this torture chamber."

"Well, you certainly can't sleep in it," she pointed out. "You'll be so stiff in the morning, you won't be able to move."

"True," he agreed. "You do have a point. There is another solution, though. The bed over the cab is a queen-size. It's certainly large enough for two adults to share without crowding each other. I'm game if you are."

He made the offer so innocently that Rainey almost found herself agreeing before she realized what he'd said. Another man, she most definitely would have put in his place. Buck, however, wasn't another man. Instead, she found herself grinning in appreciation. "You know, you're really good. How often does that work for you?"

He didn't pretend to misunderstand her. Wicked humor glinting in his eyes, he shrugged. "Depends on the woman. I guess that means no?"

She just looked at him. "What do you think?"

"You can't blame a man for trying." His smile fading, he added seriously, "The bed really is big enough for two, Rainey. And you know I was teasing. I wouldn't take advantage of you."

How many times had she heard that line? Dozens? Thousands? Over the years, she'd run into countless scoundrels and treasure hunters after the same treasure she was who'd been only too quick to promise her she could trust them. She'd learned very quickly that when a man had to promise he could be trusted, it was time to run hard and fast in the opposite direction.

Buck Wyatt wasn't one of those men.

Don't kid yourself, the voice in her head drawled. *Every man is that kind of man.*

There was a time, right after her divorce, when she'd truly believed that. But she'd been bitter, disillusioned, disappointed in herself for not realizing sooner what kind of man Carl was. With time, she'd forgiven herself, and even Carl. Did that mean she wanted to get married again? God, no! But she'd come to appreciate that maybe there were a few good men out there, men like her father and his friends, who stood by their word and wouldn't dream of taking advantage of a woman, any woman, young, old or anything in between. She just didn't meet very many of them.

Every instinct she had told her that Buck was one of those men. There was just something about him…the way he looked her straight in the eye when he met her, the firm shake of his hand when they made a deal, the way he didn't make a pass when she fell in his arms. He gave every appearance of being a man with principles, and when he promised he wouldn't touch her if she shared a bed with him, she believed him.

It was herself she wasn't sure of.

Startled by the direction of her thoughts, she stiffened. Where had that come from? She'd never met a man she couldn't trust herself with. Even with Carl, she'd always known exactly what she was doing. But when Buck touched her, when his arms slipped around her when she'd fallen, she'd felt something she'd never felt before, something that stole her breath and set her heart tripping, something that scared her and fascinated her and left her totally breathless. And she didn't have a clue what she was going to do about it.

Confused, needing space to think, there was no place to go except to bed. Alone! "I appreciate the offer," she said. "But I'll be fine. If I'm not, I'll let you know."

He wanted to argue with her—she could see it in his eyes—but he didn't push her. "No problem," he said easily, rolling out of bed and coming to his feet right next to her. "Now that we've got that settled, we both need to go to bed if we want to get an early start in the morning. Okay?"

The camper was so small that they were practically touching. Her heart pounding, she nodded, looking anywhere but at his bare chest. If she swayed the slightest bit, she would be in his arms—

"Rainey? Are you all right?"

Frowning, trying to clear her head, she swallowed a groan. *All right?* Was he serious? Of course she wasn't all right! He had her thoughts in a whirl and her senses spinning, and she couldn't seem to clear her head.

"I'm tired," she said thickly, and prayed it was true. "I just need to get some sleep."

"Then crawl into bed," he retorted. "I'll get the light."

The words were hardly out of his mouth when he hit the light switch, shrouding them in darkness. Crawling into the smaller bed, Rainey slipped into the sleeping bag that Buck had just vacated and sighed in relief— only to have the clean, male scent of him surround her as surely as his arms had earlier. It was, she decided with a silent groan, going to be a long night.

The morning dawned cold and clear, with no sign of the rain that had passed through the previous evening. His hands buried in the pockets of his jacket, Buck watched the sun rise over the rolling plains that had belonged to his family for generations, decades before he was even a gleam in his parents' eye. All his life, he'd tried to picture what the ranch looked like, smelled like, but nothing he'd imagined had prepared him for what was. Had his ancestors appreciated the silent majesty of sunrise on a cold spring morning? he wondered. How could they not? He could watch that same sunrise day after day, for the rest of his life, and never have it grow old.

"It's beautiful, isn't it?"

Caught up in his musings, he turned with a start to find Rainey standing in the open doorway of the camper, watching him. She'd changed into jeans and a midnight-blue turtleneck and sturdy boots. She was ready to hike, but he found himself missing her flannel pajamas.

Tempted to tease her, he turned back instead to the sunrise. "There's nothing like this in London."

"No, there's not."

"I didn't expect it to get to me like this," he admitted gruffly. "It must be something in my DNA. The second I stepped foot on the ranch, I felt like I was home. Then I saw my first sunrise, and I knew it."

"Do your sisters feel the same way?"

He grinned. "Let's just say they're city girls."

"And not early risers?"

"God, no!" he laughed. "I doubt that any of them have ever seen a sunrise—unless they stayed up all night."

"Then they don't know what they're missing," she said simply. "It's the only way to start the day."

"Speaking of starting the day," he said, "we're burning daylight, and there's precious little of it this time of year. But first things first. Breakfast. I believe I owe you one. What'll it be?"

"As long as I have coffee, I can get by on a slice of bread and a cold piece of bologna," she retorted.

"Bologna? What kind of creature are you?"

She laughed at his look of horror. "That's not any worse than eating kippers for breakfast. Yuck! Who thought that up?"

Refusing to be drawn into that discussion, he lifted a dark brow in that way that always made her want to smile. "Do you really want to compare the eating habits of our two countries? At least we don't eat fried Twinkies!"

"And that's something to brag about? You don't even know what you're missing! I'll bet you don't have chocolate-covered Oreos, either. Or funnel cakes! Or hot Cheetos—"

He chuckled as she launched into every conceivable snack food she could think of. "If you're going to keep this up, we're going to have to drive back into town for breakfast," he told her with dancing eyes. "You're making me hungry. I thought you'd want bacon and eggs or pancakes, maybe even Pop Tarts."

"Now you're talking sense! Why didn't you say so? Let's eat!"

Laughing, he joined her in the camper, pulled out the Pop-Tarts, then heated water on the stove for instant coffee. It wasn't the best breakfast either one of them had ever had, but it was filling and quick, and less than fifteen minutes later, they were ready to once again look for the mine.

By unspoken agreement, they headed northwest, where the canyons were steeper and it was virtually impossible to drive to. They'd packed light, carrying nothing but the turkey sandwiches he'd offered last night, fruit and water, but the going was still rough. And slow. The cedars were so thick in places that they were impenetrable. Left with no choice, they were forced to go around them. It took over an hour to reach the first canyon. Not surprisingly, it looked nothing like it had from the air.

Hesitating beside Buck as they studied the long canyon that branched to the north, Rainey frowned. "This doesn't look right. Are you sure that this is the one that turns west at the end? That was a really short canyon."

"It only looked that way from the air," he assured her. "This is it, Rainey. I'm sure of it."

She wasn't. She usually had an excellent sense of direction, but camp was hardly out of sight when clouds moved in, obscuring the sun, and she got completely turned around. Even with a compass, she felt like they'd stepped into a maze and there was no way out.

"If you say so," she said, "but this is crazy. No wonder the Spaniards marked the entrance to the canyon."

"The clouds are throwing you off," he told her. "Without the sun to guide you, it's easy to lose your way." Glancing up at the sky, he frowned. "It looks like there's another storm blowing in."

Huddling in her jacket, she said, "The temperature's dropping, too. It looks like snow."

"Hopefully, it'll hold off until later in the day," he said grimly. "We'd better get moving."

Rainey wasn't surprised that he didn't turn into the canyon, but instead began searching the entrance instead. It easily covered a hundred acres and was thick with trees. There wasn't, however, a single cedar that was even close to ten years old, let alone two hundred.

"This can't be it," she said after an hour of searching. "Unless the cedar the Spanish planted died."

"Or the Spanish didn't consider this the entrance to the canyon," he argued. Checking the rough map he'd drawn during their aerial survey of the area, he frowned. "Another canyon cuts into this one at the northern end. It runs east and west—"

"What about a stream?"

"There's a small dry stream bed that runs on the north side of the canyon," he replied. "Let's check it out."

They struck off through the trees, but the going wasn't easy. The terrain was rough and rocky, littered with fallen trees and boulders that continually blocked their path. And with every step, the clouds overhead grew darker. Their eyes on where they were putting their feet, they never noticed.

Then the first snowflakes began to fall.

"Damn! It's March! Somebody forgot to tell the weatherman!" Swearing, Buck stopped in his tracks and looked back the way they had come. A fine dusting of snow already covered their tracks. "Maybe we'd better head back. We're miles from camp. We don't want to get trapped out here in this."

"It can't be that much farther to the canyon," she argued. "We're here. Another half hour or so isn't going to make that much difference."

He hesitated. "All right. I'll give you a half hour," he said finally. "If we don't reach the canyon by then, too bad. We're done for the day. Agreed?"

"Agreed."

She stepped over a fallen tree and headed farther down the canyon. Two steps behind her, he kept his eye on the falling snow. Twenty minutes later, just as she'd predicted, they stumbled across the connecting canyon.

It only took a quick look around for Rainey to see that the cedars that grew among the rocks and pines were little more than saplings. Still, she wasn't discouraged. All the other conditions were right.

"I don't think we need to be concerned about the cedar," she told Buck. "It could have been destroyed in a forest fire or died from disease or some wandering cowboy or Indian could have used it for firewood decades ago. That doesn't mean the bell's not here. Look! There's the dry creek bed!"

Hugging the far side of the canyon, a narrow, dry creek bed cut its way through the rocks and trees, and it was impossible to tell how long it'd been since it held water. There were dozens of dry creek beds just like it all over the ranch.

Buck didn't think the bell was there, but Rainey was right about one thing—they were there, and it would be foolish not to check it out. "I'll take the right side of the canyon," he told her. "You take the left. Make it quick. We're going to have a difficult time making it back as it is."

Over the course of the last twenty minutes, the weather had worsened considerably—they had little time to waste. The canyon, however, wasn't very large, and within fifteen minutes, they had thoroughly searched it. If there was a bell there, they found no sign of it.

"We knew it wouldn't be easy," Buck told her. "It's been missing for over two hundred years. For all we know, it was lost in the avalanche, too. If that's the case, we'll never find it."

"No, it's out there," she insisted, refusing to think otherwise.

"You can't be sure of that."

"No," she agreed, "but I'd bet money on it. I've been in this business a long time, Buck. You develop a sixth sense about these things after a while. The bell is out there somewhere in these canyons, just waiting to be found."

"I hope you're right," he told her. "But we'll have to look for it another day. Right now, we've got bigger problems."

His expression carved in somber lines, he nodded in the direction behind her, back the way they'd come. The clouds had thickened and darkened, and the snow that had been falling at a steady rate since they entered the first canyon had turned into a near blizzard. With everything shrouded in white, it was impossible to tell which way they had come.

Chapter 9

Her gaze following his, Rainey gasped. "Oh my God! We've got to get back to camp!"

"We're only a couple of kilometers away," he assured her. "There's no need to panic. We'll be fine."

She didn't panic, but she had no intention of dragging her feet, either. And neither did Buck. They moved at a tight clip, keeping one eye on where they were putting their feet and the other on the worsening weather. And all the while, the snow kept falling.

They were still half a mile from the camper when the wind picked up, blowing the falling snow in their faces and making it nearly impossible to see. Swearing, Buck stopped only long enough to take Rainey's hand. "Okay?" he asked gruffly.

Winded from the brisk hike, her heart slamming against her ribs, she couldn't have answered him right then if her life had depended on it. He was covered in snow from head to toe—even his eyebrows were thick with the white stuff—and he had to be as cold as she. But the second his hand closed around hers, her blood warmed, her heart jumped, and all she could think of was how safe she felt. She nodded.

"Almost there," he told her. "I think I see the camper."

Peering around him, she didn't see anything that resembled the camper in the near-whiteout conditions. Then she caught a glimpse of the truck. She could just make out its green paint half-buried in the distance.

"I want coffee," she told Buck as they picked up the pace. "Lots and lots of coffee!"

"I'll put a pot on the second we get inside," he promised her. "Hang on. We're almost there."

Long minutes later, they stumbled inside and sighed in relief as the warmth of the camper closed around them. Buck had left the heater on low, and even though the temperature inside was in the mid sixties, it felt fifty degrees warmer than outside. Almost immediately, they began to peel off their wet jackets.

"The coffee's instant," he warned her, "but there's plenty of it. I'll change out here while you're in the bathroom, then put some water on to boil."

"Instant's fine," she assured him as she quickly gathered clean clothes. "Right now, I feel like I could drink a gallon of it. I can't remember the last time I was this cold."

Buck had to agree with her. The storm had caught him off guard, and as he changed into dry jeans and a flannel shirt, he found himself wondering how long it would snow. The truck had four-wheel drive—unless there was a hell of a blizzard, they wouldn't have any trouble getting back to the homestead. There were, however, other things to worry about. Like how long the propane would last when the heater was running nonstop. David kept the thing filled, but he'd never told him how long a tank of propane would last when it was being used around the clock.

Caught up in his musings, he was giving serious consideration to cutting the thermostat down when Rainey stepped out of the bathroom. He took one look at her and completely forgot about the propane.

She was dressed in black jeans and a red ribbed turtleneck that hugged her breasts and took his breath away. The hours they'd spent hiking the canyon had whipped color into her cheeks, and with her dark, damp hair curling around her shoulders, she looked so pretty, he couldn't take his eyes off her.

"Better?" he asked hoarsely.

"Oh, yes, thank you!" she breathed. "I just didn't realize how cold I was until I stepped into the camper and the warm air hit me. Did you change? Good. How about the coffee? Is the water ready?"

On cue, the teakettle on the stove whistled. Buck laughed. "Looks like your timing's perfect."

He spooned instant coffee into two mugs, then added

water to both. "Sugar's in the cabinet behind you," he told her as he handed her one of the mugs. "Milk's in the fridge if you need it."

When she eased past him to get to the stove, the touch of her body against his was barely more than a brush of clothes against clothes. Another man might not even have noticed it, but Buck felt the heat of it all the way to his toes. Just that easily, his blood heated and all he could think about was how close she was, how small the camper was, how much he wanted her.

He was, he decided, losing his mind.

"Buck? Hello? Where'd you go?"

Jerking back to his surrounding, he glanced up from his thoughts to find her watching him curiously, her blue eyes bright with amusement in the fading light of the camper. He should have made some quip and turned the discussion to the mine or the weather or her adventures with her father. But he couldn't take his eyes off her face. No woman had a right to look so gorgeous without makeup.

"Was it something I said?" she teased. "You're looking at me like you've never seen me before."

He blinked...and would have sworn he was blushing. What the devil was wrong with him? "I was just thinking about the mine," he lied. "I want to go over your notes again after dinner. Maybe we missed something."

"All right," she agreed, "but I've been researching the mine on and off for the last fifteen years. I'll be the first to admit that something could have slipped past me, but I've gone over my notes a million times."

"That's why I'd like to look at them. Sometimes you can miss something that's right in front of your nose. It's just better to have a second set of eyes."

"I'll do that while you're cooking dinner," she said easily, then grinned. "You are cooking, aren't you? It seems to me you agreed to two dinners and a breakfast after you welsh—"

"I didn't welsh!"

"I still don't have my steak."

"Okay," he groaned, fighting a smile, "you win. I'll cook your bloody steak. But I'll have to broil it," he warned. "You can't expect me to grill in the middle of a snowstorm."

Flashing him a wide-eyed innocent look, she said, "Of course not. I would never—"

"Yeah, right," he snorted, his lips twitching. "Don't give me that. I know your kind. You whine and grumble and set a poor man up—"

"I never...!"

"Not that I would throw that in your face," he said regally. "I'm a British gentlemen. I would never do such a thing to a woman. Even if she doesn't play by the rules."

"Oh, really?" Rainey laughed. "I'm sure she's relieved."

"But she knows who she is," he retorted, grinning. "And her days are numbered."

He was teasing, but he didn't have a clue just how true that remark was. Her days were numbered. Every time he teased her, touched her, grinned at her, the unnamed yearning in her heart grew stronger. And there wasn't a darn thing she could do about it except walk away from him and the mine, and she wasn't prepared to do that. Not yet. That day would come soon enough—for now, she just had to find a way to control the crazy emotions he stirred in her so effortlessly.

"In the meantime," she said, "she intends to eat well. She'd like her steak medium well done."

Rolling his eyes, he pulled the steaks out of the refrigerator.

Not surprisingly, dinner was delicious, and the steaks were fantastic. Rainey didn't know how he managed to cook anything so incredible on a stove that wasn't much bigger than a small television, but he certainly knew what he was doing. She ate every bite.

"That was delicious," she sighed as she helped him clean off the table. "So…what's for dessert?"

For an answer, he opened a cabinet door, pulled out a bag of Oreos and gave her two.

"That's all I get?" she asked, surprised. "Just two?"

"We have to ration," he retorted with a straight face. "We don't know how long we're going to be out here. We could get snowed in."

"So you want to make sure we don't run out of cookies?" She chuckled. "Yeah, right."

"Actually," he said, sobering, "I'm more concerned about propane. Everything runs off of it—the heater and stove, even the refrigerator. And the tank's not very big. I don't want to have to go back into town for gas, not when we're already out here."

"And we don't want to run into that jerk who tried to force us off the road, either," she pointed out. "So we'll cut back on the cooking and turn the thermostat down on the heater. After all, it's not like it's thirty below or anything. We'll be fine."

"There're plenty of covers," he assured her. "And once this storm blows through, the weather's supposed to actually be pretty mild for the rest of the week. The problem is just getting from here to there."

"I'm not a hothouse flower, Buck," she told him. "I've been in much colder temperatures than this. I'm sure I'll be fine."

Hours later, long after Buck helped her convert the dinette booth into her bed, those words came back to haunt her. When she'd first burrowed into her sleeping bag, she'd convinced herself that she'd be as warm as toast. And for a while, she was. Then as midnight came and went and the temperature outside dropped lower and lower, the camper's small heater—and its lowered thermostat—couldn't combat the encroaching cold.

Lost in her dreams, she felt the chill touch her arms and shoulders first. Shivering, she pulled the covers up higher and drifted deeper into sleep. Minutes, hours later, the cold seemed to slip through the covers and brush at her legs and toes with icy fingers. Restless, cold all the way to her bones, she shifted under the covers, drowsily searching for a spot to warm her feet, but the flannel lining of her sleeping bag felt like ice and her socks did little to protect her. With a muttered oath, she climbed out of bed and blindly searched in the dark for her suitcase and another pair of socks.

She could have pulled on a dozen pairs of socks and it would have done little good. She was just too cold. Huddled under the covers again, hugging herself, she just lay there, shivering.

This was stupid, she told herself. Buck had to be as cold as she was. Why were they sleeping in separate beds? They needed to at least be sharing their body heat.

The bed really is big enough for two, Rainey. And you know I was teasing. I wouldn't take advantage of you.

His words echoed in her ears, tempting her. In the light—and heat—of day, she never would have slipped into bed with him without at least waking him and discussing the situation. But her brain was as numb and cold as the rest of her, and all she could think about was getting warm. Climbing out of bed, she hurried up the ladder in the dark, lifted the cover and eased into bed with him.

The man was like a blast furnace! Almost immediately, his heat enveloped her and warmth began to seep into her bones. Sighing in relief, she closed her eyes and drifted closer. Seconds later, she was asleep.

Later, she couldn't have said what woke her. One minute, she was toasty warm and sound asleep, and the next, all her senses were alive and humming. Frowning, she stirred…and opened her eyes to find herself face-to-face with Buck and wrapped in his arms. His eyes were dark and sleepy and trained right on her. He looked as if he'd been watching her for hours.

Startled, she stiffened. "Oh, God, I'm sorry! I should have woke you, but I hated to. I was just trying to get warm."

"No problem," he said in a raspy voice that stroked her from the top of her head all the way down to her toes. "I told you there was plenty of room for both of us."

"But I'm crowding you—"

"I know. It feels good, doesn't it?"

"Buck—"

Grinning at her warning tone, he said, "C'mon, tell the truth. There's no one here but you and me, and I'll never tell. I'll even go first. I already did."

"I should go back to my own bed."

"No, you should stay here…and kiss me."

"Oh, no!"

"Oh, yes," he growled softly, and leaned forward to kiss her softly on the lips.

She should have stopped him. She should have stopped herself. But his mouth was whisper soft against hers, tenderly seducing. Then he touched her, tracing a finger up and down her arm over and over again, and her mind clouded. With a murmur of need, she found herself sinking into him, kissing him back, and she couldn't remember why she shouldn't let him touch her, let alone kiss her. Not when it felt so good.

Outside, the night was still and icy cold, but wrapped

in each other's arms under the covers, they never noticed. He kissed her sweetly, hungrily, with ever-increasing need, making her ache. Then his hand moved to the buttons of her flannel pajama top.

Her breath caught in her throat. "Buck…"

All she wanted him to do was touch her…just touch her. But when the soft material of her pajama top parted, the only touch she felt was of the cold night air. Moaning softly, she reached for his hand.

"Patience, love," he murmured. "We have all night."

All night? Images played in her head, teasing her senses, setting her body humming. Then he kissed the side of her neck, and a shiver rippled through her body. "Oh, Buck." She sighed. "Do that again."

She felt him smile against her neck, then trace his tongue over the delicate skin of her throat. Did he know what that did to her? How hot he made her with just a kiss? She'd been fantasizing about touching him, making love with him, almost from the moment she'd first laid eyes on him. And now she was in his arms, under him, and she wanted him more than she'd ever wanted a man in her life.

But she wouldn't rush, she promised herself. Not this first time. Not when she could drag out the pleasure and drive them both crazy.

"Whatever you want, love," he rasped, and kissed the side of her neck again.

This time, however, he didn't stop there. Kissing her, distracting her, he peeled back each side of her pajama top with painstaking slowness, revealing her naked breasts in the pale moonlight that glinted through the camper's bunk window. This time, he was the one who caught his breath. Then he reached out and traced her nipple with a touch that was as soft as a feather.

With a startled cry, she arched under him. "Buck... please!"

Just that easily, she broke his control. With a murmur that was her name, he moved over her, kissing his way down to one breast, then another, easing her clothes from her, only to groan when her hands moved over his bare chest, then down to his pajama bottoms, stroking, caressing every inch of him, driving him crazy.

There was no time for teasing after that, no time for thought, for anything but the need that burned between them like an inferno deep inside her. And with every sigh, every moan, every groan he pulled from her, the fire grew hotter, more intense.

Her breath tearing through her lungs, the roar of her blood loud in her ears, Rainey had never felt so desired in her life. With his hands and mouth, he discovered every sensitive spot on her body, then set out to make her so desperate for release that she couldn't remember her own name. It was mad, wonderful, mindless. And when he moved with her, in her, driving her higher and higher, it was his name she cried when she came apart in his arms.

Chapter 10

She was falling in love with him.

Long after Buck rolled over and fell asleep, the thought crept up on Rainey in the dark and wrapped around her heart. Stunned, she told herself her imagination was playing tricks on her. She couldn't possibly be in love. She wasn't looking for a man, didn't want one. Especially one like Buck. He was…

Wonderful. Considerate. Generous. Incredibly tender and giving.

And she was losing her mind.

Shaken, she dragged in a quiet, bracing breath, but it didn't help. Her heart was thundering in her breast, and suddenly, all she wanted to do was cry. And that stunned her. She couldn't remember the last man who'd tied her emotions in knots and brought her to tears just by existing. It certainly hadn't been Carl. At the time she'd married him, she'd have sworn she loved him more than life itself, but just thinking about loving him had never come close to bringing her to tears. By the time they'd divorced, all she could think about was getting her career and life back and never making that kind of mistake again.

So what was she doing? How could she even think she was falling in love again? She knew the dangers, the pitfalls, the heartache. Did she really want to chance going through that all over again?

You don't know that it's going to end in heartache, the voice in her head said sharply. *He's nothing like Carl. And you're not the same woman you were back then. You've been alone a long time. Do you really want to go through the rest of your life by yourself? What about children?*

All too easily, she could see a little boy with Buck's eyes and her curly black hair. And a sister, she thought, smiling. Her little boy would need a baby sister with rosy cheeks and sparkling blue eyes and a smile full of mischief. She could see them now, laughing and playing with Buck, running to her, jumping into her arms....

Children, she thought, dazed. Why hadn't she realized she wanted children? A family? A home? How long had she been burying her feelings without even knowing it?

Still reeling, she needed some time to herself, some

time to think, to sort out the emotions that were suddenly swirling inside her like a whirlwind. But it was the middle of the night, and she had to crawl over Buck to get out of bed. If she woke him—and the odds were that she would—she knew they would make love again.

Her heart turned over at the thought. No! she told herself fiercely. She wasn't going there, not until she had a handle on the emotions he stirred in her. She had to think. But how could she when he was so close that he warmed her toes without even touching her? And then there was the raw male scent of him that she drew in with every breath she took. How was a woman supposed to think clearly when a man completely bombarded her senses?

Stuck, there was nothing she could do but lie next to him in the dark and wait for morning.

It was a long night.

The sun was just a glow on the eastern horizon when she knew she couldn't lie there another second. Lightning quick, she climbed over him and was on the first rung of the ladder, blindly searching for the second, when a strong male hand closed around her wrist.

Startled, she almost fell off the ladder. "What…!"

"Where're you going? Come back to bed."

His rough growl stroked her like a caress, weakening her knees. Swallowing a moan, she hesitated, so tempted she could already taste his kiss. Did he know what he was doing to her? How he only had to touch her—

Stiffening at her thoughts, she mentally shook her

head. No. She couldn't do this. She had to get her emotions under control. Now! Pulling free of his touch, she said lightly, "The sun's up. Time to get up. I was thinking we could cook outside this morning. The storm's blown itself out, and it looks like it's going to be a beautiful day."

"All right," he said, studying her with a frown. "I'll start a campfire. You sure want to cook? I don't mind doing it."

"Oh, no," she assured him. "I want to. Really. I've always loved cooking on a campfire. My grandmother taught me how to make biscuits in a Dutch oven when I was twelve and I've been doing it ever since."

"Then I'll start the fire while you're getting dressed," he said easily. "Take your time. I'll call you when it's ready."

Relieved, Rainey grabbed her jeans and sweatshirt, but she knew she'd only temporarily dodged a bullet. What was she going to do tonight?

What was going on in her head?

Traipsing through another one of the ranch's countless canyons, Buck watched Rainey as she searched the right side of the canyon for the dry creek bed they'd seen from the air. She'd chatted on and off throughout the morning as if nothing the least bit intimate had happened between them, but Buck wasn't fooled. He'd held her in his arms, kissed her, made love to her and lost himself in her, and he knew for a fact that she was far from indifferent where he was concerned. So why was she acting as if last night never happened? Who did she think she was fooling?

Frustrated—and more than a little irritated—he was tempted to grab her and kiss her senseless just to see if she could ignore that, but he couldn't, dammit! He didn't know what was going on with her, but he wasn't the kind of man who forced himself on a woman. And she obviously needed some space. He could give her that.

"Hey," he called to her. "Did you find anything?"

"Not yet," she called back. "What about you?"

"Nothing. I think we're wasting our time here." Heading toward her, he said, "What do you think about moving on? Or do you want to go deeper into the canyon?"

Studying the long, narrow canyon, she shook her head. "No, you're right. It just doesn't look right. The records I found in Spain described the creek as a deep flowing creek that was as wide as the mast of a ship."

"It could have narrowed over the years…or dried up completely."

"True," she agreed. "But the creek bed I found near the canyon wall isn't even six feet wide. And it doesn't look like it was ever wider than that."

"Then let's move on," he said. "We'll need to move camp more to the west. We've gone as far as we can from here."

"But what about the rocks?"

"We'll head south and try to pick our way around them. If that doesn't work, then we'll hike in as far as we can. That's the best we can do, Rainey. The only other solution is to come back another time and bring horses and go up into the high country. And who knows? Maybe the mine isn't really in a canyon at all. Or what the Spaniards called a canyon isn't what we call a canyon."

"Anything's possible," she agreed. "For what it's worth, I checked the translation, and the meaning hasn't changed over the centuries. That doesn't mean, however, that the description I found wasn't written in code."

He grinned. "Truc. It's all a crapshoot. All we can do is keep looking and hope we get lucky."

He didn't push her to talk about last night; he didn't even try to touch her. They hiked back to where they'd left the camper, then spent the next two hours finding their way through the rocks and rough terrain that made the western edge of the Broken Arrow so inaccessible to motorized vehicles, and not once did Buck do anything to make her feel uncomfortable. He talked and laughed and treated her as if she were his sister or something. She should have been pleased. Wasn't this what she wanted? So why was she so irritated?

"This is the end of the road…at least for today."

Lost in her thoughts, Rainey blinked and only just then realized he had braked to a stop before a thick stand of trees blocking their path. And the sun was still fairly high in the sky. "You're stopping now? But why? It's still early." And she wasn't ready to even think about bedtime—and sharing a bed with him

"We don't know how long it'll take to get around these trees," he replied, cutting the engine. "And it's a good time to stop. I thought I'd build a campfire and grill some pork chops."

A campfire, she thought in relief. They could spend hours sitting around a campfire, talking, staring at the stars. "That's a great idea. I'll go get some wood."

"I'll help you—"

"That's okay. I can do it while you're digging the fire pit."

He started to argue, only to hesitate. "All right. Yell if you need some help."

"I will," she promised, and hurried into the trees in search of kindling and fallen branches. The pounding of her heart loud in her ears, she could almost feel his eyes on her as she walked away, but he made no move to stop her. Did he realize that she had to make herself put some space between them? That she couldn't stop thinking about last night? That, more than anything, she wanted to throw caution to the wind and just enjoy what time she had left with him? No strings, no promises, no future. Just today…and tonight. What was wrong with that?

Nothing, her heart retorted, *as long as you don't do something stupid like fall in love with the man. Remember…he was engaged just a few months ago, and his ex was the one who ended their engagement. Do you really think the feelings he had for her died that quickly? Watch yourself, or you're the one who's going to end up with a broken heart.*

She was determined that wasn't going to happen.

After her divorce, it had taken only a matter of months to put Carl and all the hurt and resentment he had stirred in her behind her. Buck, however, wasn't Carl. If she made the mistake of falling in love with him, she didn't know if she would ever get over losing him.

When pain squeezed her heart at the thought, she stiffened. What, she wondered wildly, was she doing? She was supposed to be collecting firewood, not daydreaming about Buck. Dragging her attention back to the task at hand, she frowned at the ground in front of her feet and began collecting small branches and limbs that had fallen from the pines that towered overhead.

Mindlessly lost in her task, she filled her arms in just a matter of minutes. She should have headed back to camp, but she really wasn't ready to face Buck—and her feelings—yet. So she searched for a few more pieces of wood that were just the right size, and in the process, never saw the boulder that was rolling down the hill toward her until it was almost upon her.

"Ohhh!" Horrified, she jumped out of the way, and the wood she was carrying went flying. Before she could do anything but gasp, she found herself sliding down the hill.

Panicking, she tried to catch herself, but the hill was steeper than she'd realized and in the time it took to blink, the trees were whizzing past. And at the bottom of the hill, the boulder that had nearly flattened her sat right in her path, waiting for her.

There was no time to think. Her heart in her throat,

she threw herself to the right just seconds before she would have slammed into the rock. Dirt and pine needles and a sprinkling of snow hit her in the face. Her right shoulder grazed a tree stump, and she thought she heard her pants rip. When she finally shuddered to a stop, she was face-first on the rough ground and just inches from the boulder.

Later, she couldn't have said how long she lay there, trying to catch her breath, waiting for the roar of her blood in her ears to ease. That was close, she thought, shaken. Too close. Taking a mental inventory of her body parts, she sent up a silent prayer of thanks that nothing seemed to be broken. Oh, she was sure every bone in her body would be aching before the day was over with, but overall, she was lucky to escape with nothing more than a few aches and pains.

Groaning, she pushed herself out of the dirt and snow and gingerly climbed to her feet, brushing herself off as she scowled up the hill. How the devil had a boulder come loose? Granted, the ground was still damp from the rain and snow that fell over the course of the last week, but she wouldn't have thought that would have loosened it enough to send it rolling down the hill. But then again, there were a lot of rocks at the bottom of the hill.

Realizing her firewood had also tumbled down the hill and was scattered all around her, she stepped over to where several medium-size logs had landed and leaned down to pick one up. That's when she saw the bell half-buried in the snow.

Stunned, she just stood there, half-bent over, staring at the mission bell that was centuries old. It couldn't be, she thought, dazed. She couldn't have found it so easily. She was just looking for firewood, and there it was.

It hit her then—she'd found the bell! The mine had to be somewhere nearby.

"Oh my God!" Straightening abruptly, she laughed... and cried and whirled to run toward camp. She'd only taken two steps, however, when she stopped in her tracks. What was she doing? She couldn't leave and risk losing it again. And she couldn't move it by herself.

"Buck! BUCK!"

In the middle of digging a firepit big enough to roast an elephant, Buck had just stopped to wipe the sweat from his brow when he thought he heard Rainey scream. Then he heard her again. Before he even thought to note which direction she'd gone, he took off running.

"Oh my God! I can't believe it! I can't believe it! BUCK! Where are you?"

"Here!" he panted, half sliding down the hill toward her. His heart slamming against his ribs, he grabbed her as she launched herself at him. "Are you all right? What's going on? I could hear you screaming half a county away!"

"The bell!" She laughed, kissing him fiercely. "I found the bell. Look!"

Grabbing his hand, she pulled him after her over the uneven ground, uncaring that she was covered in dirt and her jeans were torn at the knee. "I fell," she told him breathlessly. "The rock was careening down the hill—"

"*What?*"

"I'm okay," she assured him, laughing. "I—" She sobered, her eyes wide with shock. "Oh, my God!"

"What? Dammit, talk to me!"

"The curse," she gasped. "The boulder came out of nowhere, and the next thing I knew, I was on my face in the snow and the bell was just a few steps away. Look."

Dropping to her knees, she pulled him down beside her. And there in front of them, less than two feet in front of them, was the bell that adventurers and treasure hunters had been looking for for centuries.

Buck took one look at it and didn't doubt for a second that it was the original mission bell. Aside from the fact that it appeared to be hundreds of years old, the writing around its lip was in Italian, not Spanish, just as Rainey had discovered in her research. This had to be it.

Feeling as if he'd been hit in the head with a rock, he sat back on his heels and just looked at her. "I can't believe you found it. I was beginning to think the mine was nothing but a lie that someone had started back in the eighteenth century as some kind of joke. Dammit, Rainey, no one's seen this thing since the 1700s! Do you know what this means? You found the mine!"

"Not yet—"

He didn't give her time to argue further, but simply surged to his feet with a laugh and pulled her into his arms for a fierce hug. "You did it! I still can't believe it.

I didn't tell you, but I never really thought we'd ever find it. What were the odds? A zillion to one? Think about it. How many people have looked for the mine over the centuries? It's got to be thousands. And no one even knew about the bell, let alone stumbled across it, until you tripped and fell down a hill. Do you know how incredible that is?"

"It was just dumb luck," she said, blushing. "It could have happened to anyone."

"No, it couldn't have," he argued. "Everyone else was looking in the wrong place."

"Well, yes, that's true. But—"

"But nothing," he retorted. "You did your homework and it paid off. Let's go look for the mine, then we'll come back for the bell before we return to camp."

He expected her to jump at the chance. Instead, she hesitated. "What?" he asked, alarmed. "What's the problem now?"

"The curse," she retorted. "I'm telling you, Buck, that boulder was heading right toward me."

"What do you mean…it was heading right toward you? Where'd it come from?"

"Up the hill," she said, nodding toward a stand of trees up the hill from them. "If I hadn't heard it and looked up, it would have flattened me."

"Let's check it out," he growled, and strode quickly up the hill to the trees.

Buck didn't believe in curses…or coincidence. If that boulder rolled down the hill at the exact moment that Rainey was in its path, then someone must have pushed it.

But when he reached the spot where the boulder had obviously rested for decades, there was no sign that something—or *someone*—had knocked it loose. There were no footprints, no signs that the ground around where the rock had rested had been tampered with.

Breathless, Rainey reached his side and frowned down at the spot where the boulder had been only moments before. "Well? See anything?"

"No," he retorted, and shot her a sharp look. "Tell me again what happened."

She described the moment when she'd looked up and seen a rock the size of Manhattan heading right for her. "It just seemed to come out of nowhere. If I hadn't jumped out of the way, it would have killed me. That's when I fell and rolled down the hill."

"And found the bell," he said grimly.

She nodded. "I'm telling you, Buck, I'm afraid that curse is for real. I know you think it's just a tall tale that someone came up with in order to keep thieves away, but what if it's not? What if there's some truth to it? Shouldn't we at least do something to protect ourselves?"

Frowning, he lifted a dark brow at her. "Like what? Wear a dead cat's foot around our necks? Or sprinkle chicken blood on the ground around the bell?"

"No, of course not!"

"Then what, love? Just how do you protect yourself from a superstition? Drink from the wrong side of a glass or what? Not that there is a wrong side of a glass," he added. "At least not that I know of. But I could be wrong. I'm not into spells and curses and all this Harry Potter stuff."

"You have to admit that there are things in this world we don't understand," she pointed out.

"So you really believe this was a result of the curse?"

"I'm just saying there's nothing wrong with having a healthy respect for a power you can't explain. And a smart person would do what they could to protect themselves. Just in case."

He grinned. "I agree completely, love. I, too, believe in *just in case*. So what do you suggest we do in this situation? Because curse or no curse, nothing is going to stop me from looking for the mine now that you've found the bell."

Startled that he might think she wouldn't be in total agreement with that, she said, "Of course we're going to look for it. I just need to sprinkle a little weegone weed around the bell."

He just looked at her. "*Weegone* weed?"

"It's just something I picked up from a medicine man in the wilds of the Congo. And, yes, it works."

She was serious, Buck thought, amazed. How could a bright, beautiful, intelligent woman believe in something called weegone weed? "Whatever you say, love. Sprinkle away."

A blush stung her cheeks, but she didn't let his teasing stop her from pulling a small vial from her pocket and tapping out a minuscule amount of white powder around the bell. When she was finished, she surveyed her handiwork critically, then nodded, satisfied. "Okay, we can look for the mine now."

"You're sure we're safe?"

She gave him a withering look that was totally ruined by the smile she couldn't hold back. "Go ahead and laugh. You can thank me later, when nothing goes wrong."

"I'll do that," he promised, chuckling. "If that stuff works, I'm going to order a case of it and sprinkle it all over the ranch."

Turning his back on the bell, he looked directly across the canyon, which was where the mine was supposedly located. Frowning, he said, "See anything that looks like a landslide? It's got to be around here somewhere."

They both surveyed the far side of the canyon, but if they thought they were going to find the mine as easily as they had located the bell, they quickly realized that wasn't going to happen. The south wall of the canyon was a series of steep, graduated hills that seemed to run the entire length of the canyon. Thick with brush, it was impossible to tell if part or all of it had been caused by an avalanche or where the original canyon wall had been.

"Looks like we've got our work cut out for us," he said grimly. "C'mon. Let's see what we can find."

Already two steps ahead of him, Rainey couldn't stop smiling. There was nothing more exhilarating than finding a treasure—she'd been a treasure hunter for most of her life and the high of finding something that had been lost for centuries never got old. But this was different. More than any other treasure on earth, this was the one her father had longed to find. And now she was finding it for him. She wanted to cry, to laugh, to walk on air.

Catching up with her in two long strides, Buck shot her a grin. "You're looking awfully pleased with yourself."

"I am."

"We haven't found the mine yet, you know. Don't count your chickens just yet."

"I'm not," she assured him. "But we're so close! If you close your eyes and listen, you can almost hear the wagons wheels as the Spanish missionaries hauled the ore out of the mine and carted it back to town. How did they even find this place?"

"Probably the same way we did," he said dryly. "There's not too many ways through these canyons. They probably camped here for the night and stumbled across some ore in the creek bed when they were getting water, and realized there was gold somewhere nearby. Their ghosts are long gone, Rainey."

Stopping in her tracks to study the lay of the land, she smiled softly. "No, they're not. I can feel them."

"That's the wind, love, kissing your cheeks. There's no one here but you and me."

Far from discouraged, she only grinned. "You obviously have no romance in your soul."

"Are you kidding? I grew up in England, reading stories about cowboys and Indians. I'm just as much an adventurer as you are, Rainey, just in a different way."

She hadn't thought of him in that way, but she had to agree. Only someone with the soul of an adventurer would walk away from his life in England to live on a ranch in the wilds of Colorado.

"I stand corrected," she replied with twinkling eyes. "So, Mr. Adventurer, where do we start?"

"Since we're not sure which of the hills that form the southern wall of the canyon were a result of the avalanche and which were there beforehand, the most logical way to conduct the search is to just start at the bell and head straight across the canyon. The bell's supposed to be even with the entrance to the mine, right?"

She nodded. "The diary notes were pretty clear. The bell marked the entrance to the mine."

"Then it has to be somewhere close by. For all we know, it could be right under our feet, buried under thousands of tons of rock and dirt. If we don't find anything, then I'll have to bring in a bulldozer to haul out some of this dirt."

"And if we don't find it?"

"Then we keep digging. We will find it, Rainey," he told her quietly. "It's just a matter of time."

Reassured, she grinned. "You're damn straight we're going to find it. We didn't get this close to walk away now."

An hour before sunset, they were left with no choice but to call it a day and return to camp. They hadn't uncovered anything that even hinted at where the entrance to the mine was, but Rainey was far from discouraged. "What's the first thing you're going to buy when the money comes in on the mine?" she asked Buck as he laid a fire in the firepit with the wood they'd gathered on their way back to camp.

Looking up from his task, he shot her a grin. "You're counting your chickens, Rainey."

"I know." She chuckled. "But I've never hit it this big before. What percentage did we agree on? Twenty-five?"

"Nice try," he laughed. "I believe it was more like one percent."

"Oh, no, it wasn't! This was a sure thing. If I remember correctly, it was twelve percent of gross."

"I must have been out of my mind," he teased. "It was only dumb luck that you found the bell, anyway. If you hadn't fallen—"

"I prefer to think of that as pure skill," she cut in loftily, making no attempt to hold back a smile. "Think about it. People have been looking for the bell for centuries. How many of them fell right in front of it? That takes talent."

"Or two left feet."

Far from offended, she only laughed. "You're just ticked because I was right. You really didn't think we'd find it, did you?"

"No," he said honestly, grinning. "We got lucky…or you got klutzy. So what are you going to do with your finder's fee?"

"I don't know. I always thought that if I ever got a big payoff, I'd use the money to check out some sunken ships off the coast of the Bahamas."

Starting the fire with a quick flick of a match, Buck sent her a searching look over the rising flames. "But now you've changed your mind."

It wasn't a question but a statement, and she couldn't deny it. "It would just be nice to have a place to go to between treasure hunts."

Surprised, he said, "You're thinking about buying a house? Are you planning on giving up treasure hunting?"

"I didn't say that," she said quickly. "I love my work. I can't imagine ever doing anything else, but the odds are that I won't be able to do this forever. People get old—"

"And decrepit."

"Buck—"

"Maybe you should see about lining up some kind of home health care. It's not too soon to think about that kind of thing, you know. You're not as young as you used to be—"

"Buck—"

"You should buy a place close to a hospital, too. Just in case you—"

He never saw the first pinecone she threw at him. Then she grinned and threw another. Surprised, he caught it, and a slow, wicked smile curled the corners of his sensuous mouth. Without a word, he threw it back. The battle was on.

Chapter 11

Jumping up from the log she'd been sitting on, she laughed and scooped up one pinecone after another, but she was laughing too much to aim properly and most of her ammunition fell well short of its mark. Buck, on the other hand, was like a machine gun, bombarding her with a rain of pinecones that had her running for cover.

"Stop! Stop!" She laughed as he ran after her. "You're killing me!"

"Too bad! You started it. Say 'uncle' and I might consider it."

"Are you kidding? What kind of pansy do you think I am?" Darting around a tree, she scooped up three large cones and turned to face him. "Take that! And that, you dog! What kind of man would attack a defenseless woman?"

"Defenseless? You? I've never met a less defenseless woman in my life! And don't you dare cry *poor me*. You started this!"

"I did not." she retorted indignantly, giggling as she darted behind a huge tree. "Just because a pinecone fell out of a tree and hit you on the nose is no reason for you to attack me. I'm totally innocent—"

Sneaking around the tree, planning to catch him off guard, she peeked around the trunk…and found herself face-to-face with him. "Gotcha!" he growled, and grabbed her.

Startled, she laughed, and just that easily, found herself in his arms. Blue eyes met blue and in the time it took to draw in a deep breath, need hit her like a punch in the gut. Her smile faded, and suddenly, all she could think of was last night and how tenderly he'd made love to her.

He felt it, too. She could see it in his eyes. "Don't look at me like that," he rasped. "Not unless you want me to take you right here and now."

Her body started to hum and he hadn't even kissed her. "Promise?"

His eyes darkened from blue to midnight black. "Witch," he groaned. "Are you trying to drive me crazy?"

A slow smile flirted with her mouth. "Is that what I'm doing?"

"You don't know the half of it, love," he groaned.

She was driving him crazy. Couldn't she tell? Last night, it seemed like hours before he'd stopped touching her. He'd fallen asleep with his hands on her, then spent the rest of the night dreaming of her. He'd promised himself he wasn't going to rush her into anything tonight, but the second he'd touched her, he'd known that was never going to happen. Not when she already had him tied in knots and he hadn't done anything more than touch her.

His gaze fell to her mouth, her soft, sensuous, sexy mouth, and before he could stop himself, he was leaning toward her, slowly, inexorably, eliminating the distance between them without ever taking his eyes from hers. Would she push him away if he kissed her…or pull him close? He had to find out.

Giving in to the need that burned like an inferno in his gut, he took her mouth in a sweet, hot kiss. She sighed into his mouth like she'd been waiting forever for him to take her into his arms and kiss her. Entranced, he pulled her closer, and loved the way she melted into him.

Hot. God, she made him hot! She kissed him as if he was the only man in the world she'd ever wanted, and just that quickly, he was on fire for her. He tried to tell himself that he needed to take it slow and easy, but her tongue rubbed along his, stoking a fire that was already raging, and he knew that he was never going to be satisfied with a few kisses. He wanted her bare against him…skin against skin…right where they stood.

But even as he reached for the hem of her sweater to

pull it over her head, the chill of the coming night touched him, reminding him that the sun was quickly going down. The temperature would soon be dropping like a rock.

He pulled back. "Stay right here," he growled, giving her a quick, fierce kiss. "I'll be right back."

Not giving her time to argue, he turned and hurried into the camper. When he returned a few minutes later, he was carrying two sleeping bags he'd zipped together and two pillows. Positioning them before the fire, he reached for her. "Now…where were we?"

If she was going to change her mind, she knew this was the time to speak up. But he held out his hand to her and looked at her with those dark blue eyes of his and she couldn't have denied him—or herself—for all the lost treasures in the world. Later, she knew she was going to have to have a serious talk with herself, but for now, there was only Buck and their waiting sleeping bags and the quietly crackling fire. Her eyes locked with his, she gave him her hand.

With nothing more than a gentle tug, he pulled her into his arms and another kiss. Then another. And all the while, his hands moved over her, finding snaps and zippers and hooks and making her body hum. She should have been cold as her clothes were pulled from her piece by piece, but when he brushed her breasts and hips and thighs with fingers that teased and tantalized, he made her burn.

Hot, restless, needing so much more, she tugged at

his clothes with growing urgency, jerking down the zipper of his jacket and pushing it from his broad shoulders in the time it took to blink. Before it hit the ground, her hands rushed to attack the buttons of his red plaid shirt and the snap of his jeans.

Kissing him desperately, she could have stripped him naked then, but his own breathing was ragged and he pushed her hands away. "Let me," he whispered, and jerked down the zipper to his jeans. A moment later, they hit the ground, along with his shirt. He was normally particular about his clothes, but at that moment, he wouldn't have cared if they'd ended up in the fire. All he wanted was Rainey.

God, she was beautiful! The firelight stroked her skin like an artist's brush, painting the dips and curves of her body in shadow and light, turning her skin to gold. Her hair tumbled around her bare shoulders, giving her a wild, sexy look, but it was the heat in her blue eyes that set his blood on fire.

"I want you," he said, reaching out to trace a nipple with just a promise of a touch. When her breath caught softly in her lungs, he smiled faintly. "You're so beautiful. So responsive. I want to touch you all over with just my fingertips and watch you come undone. I can already see it in my head, taste you on my tongue. We're both going to love it."

Her eyes closing on a trembling sigh as he moved his hand to her other nipple, she swayed toward him helplessly. "Buck—"

"But I can't."

It took a moment for his words to register. When they did, her eyes flew open in consternation. "No! You can't just stop! Not now."

His fingers left her nipple to trail slowly down the center of her naked body. "I never said anything about stopping," he growled roughly. "Just don't ask me to go slow."

And with no more warning than that, his fingers slid down her belly, drawing a gasp of surprise from her even as his mouth covered hers. She was still shuddering when he pulled her down to the sleeping bag with him.

There was no time for talking after that. Kissing her fiercely, he took her from one peak to another before she could do anything but gasp. Then when her blood was still roaring in her ears, he started all over again.

Madness. There was no other way to describe it. Moving under him, with him, around him, she sent her hands flying over him in a wild, hungry exploration, wanting more, needing more, desperate for...everything. She touched him and made him stiffen, kissed him and made him groan. And with every touch, every move, every kiss, the heat between them grew hotter.

Her mind blurring and her body humming, she wanted it to last forever, but she could already feel herself coming apart at the seams. Then, before she could do anything but cry his name, she shattered.

At her cry, Buck tried to draw the pleasure out, but he was fighting a losing battle. Need clawed at him, tying him in knots, threatening to destroy him. Sliding her hands down his back, Rainey pulled him closer, deeper into him, and just that easily, his control disintegrated. Groaning, he lost himself in her.

Sometime in the middle of the night, when the fire died and the passion cooled between them, the cold air drove them back to the camper. Wrapped in each other's arms, they made loved again, only to fall asleep still entwined.

Sated, the steady beat of his heart echoing in her ear, Rainey lay with her head against his chest and never wanted to move again. She couldn't seem to think anymore without thinking of him…his smile, the glint of wicked humor in his eyes, the way his brows knit when he was thinking. Did he know what he did to her? How safe he made her feel? How content?

Did he know that she loved him? Did he love her? What, she wondered wildly, would she do if he did?

"I think we need to go back to the house."

In the process of taking a bite of one of the biscuits she'd made in the Dutch oven for breakfast, Rainey looked up at him in surprise. "What? Why? I thought we were going to look for the mine again this morning."

"We need a bulldozer," he replied. "And help. Now that we know the general location of the mine, it shouldn't be that difficult to find. We just need the right equipment and some help."

"*Help?*" she choked out. "Are you kidding? You've got to be careful. Once the news hits the street that we've found the mine, you're going to have people coming out of the woodwork offering to help."

"I know—"

"And every single one of them will just be looking for an opportunity to rob you blind. I know what I'm talking about," she warned when he opened his mouth to object. "I've seen it happen time and time again. You've got to keep this as quiet as possible."

"I agree," he said, smiling. "I have no intention of spreading the news around town, love. I've got to call David, see how his mother's doing, when he thinks he's coming back and then make plans."

Rainey knew he was right—they needed help—but it was so difficult for her to trust people she didn't know. Especially when it came to looking for and finding lost treasure. She had nothing personal against David. She just didn't know him. Not, she reminded herself, that she'd known Buck all that well when she'd made a deal with him, but that was different. He owned the ranch, so she'd had to work with him if she wanted to find the treasure. Still, she'd have walked away from him and the ranch without a backward glance if she hadn't felt that she could trust him.

So she'd made a deal…and fallen in love.

But she wasn't going there right now, she reminded herself. She was focusing on finding the treasure. That was it. End of story. Whatever she felt for Buck—and he felt for her—would have to be dealt with later.

"You're right." She sighed. "I'm just paranoid. Blame

it on the job. I've seen too many people lose a treasure they've been looking for for years because they couldn't keep the location a secret."

"Only the three of us will know, love, at least for now, anyway. Once we actually find the opening to the mine, we'll need professional help, security, but right now, I need to know when David's coming back, and I can't call him from here. So don't worry. We'll be fine. I'm going to take care of everything."

He made it sound so easy. She just hoped he was right.

The mine was only twenty-five miles from the house, but it took an hour and a half for them to drive out of the canyons and make their way back to the two-lane road that gave the only access to the far northwest corner of the ranch. The second they reached the house, Buck called David.

"We just got back to the house," he told him, not mentioning the mine. "How's your mother doing?"

"She died last Saturday," he said stiffly.

"I'm so sorry. Are you all right? Is there anything I can do to help?"

"I've spent the last few days cleaning out her condominium—she didn't have much. And since she put everything in my name years ago, I don't have to go through probate."

"Still, it's got to be tough doing this by yourself. What about the house? Are you going to sell it or what?"

"Actually, I've already found a renter. He's bartering rent for work on the condo, so there's not much left for me to do. I'm on my way home," he added. "I should be there in a few hours."

"If you need some time off…"

"No, I'm fine," David assured him. "I need to get back to work, to take my mind off everything."

"If you're sure," Buck said. "I need your help with something. I'll see you in a couple of hours."

Hanging up, he turned to Rainey "His mother died Saturday."

"Oh, no!"

"He's on his way home and wants to work. We should have everything ready by the time he gets here."

By the time David pulled into the circular drive at the front of the house, Buck and Rainey had the bulldozer loaded onto its flatbed trailer and hitched to the truck. The camper was restocked with food, and the ranch fuel truck was full of diesel.

Stepping out of the VW he kept for runs to town, David surveyed the caravan they'd put together and frowned as Buck stepped forward to greet him. "What's going on? Where are you going with the bulldozer?"

"Up to the northwest entrance," he said. "We may have narrowed down where the mine is."

"What? You're kidding!"

"We're not sure," Buck added quickly, "but conditions look pretty darn good. I hope you don't mind—we've been using your camper to stay in so we wouldn't have to make daily trips back to the house."

"No, that's fine," he assured him. "I told you that you could use it whenever you needed to."

Buck grinned. "I've seen parts of this ranch I didn't even know existed. So how soon can you be ready to go? We're taking the bulldozer up there to see what we can find. I was hoping you'd get back so you could help us. We'll start excavating immediately."

"Well, sure," he said, surprised. "Just let me unload my things, and I'll be ready."

"We'll have to make trips back here for gas, but other than that, be prepared to stay awhile. We're not going anywhere until we find the mine.

"And that's privileged information, David," he added, sobering. "It's not to be repeated to anyone."

"Yes, sir," he said somberly. "I understand."

Rainey waited only until he was out of earshot before she turned to Buck. "You can't be serious."

"About what? About starting work immediately? You're damn straight I'm serious. Now that we've found the bell, I don't intend to take any chances that someone else may stumble across it. I want to get started on the excavation as soon as possible. We can work tonight."

"Tonight?"

"The bulldozer has lights," he said, chuckling at her reaction. "We've also got some portable lights that will illuminate the area up like a football field."

Rainey frowned. "Are you sure that's wise? The mine might be in one of the ranch's most remote areas, but lights in the middle of nowhere can be seen for miles. What if one of your neighbors—or whoever tried to drive us off the road—sees the lights and decides to investigate? You said yourself that there could be any number of people who don't want you here. If that's the case, they'll be even more determined to make sure you don't find the mine. The last thing they'll want is for you to have one more reason to stay."

"Too bad," he retorted. "We are going to find it whether they like it or not, and there's not a damn thing they can do about it."

"Except cause you a hell of a lot of trouble when you're a long way from anywhere," she pointed out. "Cell phones don't work out there, Buck. What are you going to do if someone shows up with a gun?"

"Protect myself and you and anyone who has my permission to be there," he said simply. "I'll take my rifle, Rainey. Plus there are wolves and mountain lions and even bears on the ranch. You never know what you're going to run into. I believe in being prepared."

Still not convinced, she frowned. "I'm worried about the lights. They're a dead giveaway. Can't you wait until the morning to start the excavation? We can still go out there this afternoon, then be ready to start at dawn."

"But think how much further along we'll be tomorrow if we start today," he reasoned. "If it'll make you feel better, I'll even call a security company before we leave this afternoon and start the arrangements for security. It's Friday afternoon—I doubt that we can have anyone out here before Monday, at the earliest, but at least the wheels will be in motion."

As far as plans went, it was a good one. He'd covered all his bases, and he was right—the faster he jumped on this before too many people found out, the better. By the time his enemies discovered he'd found the mine, security would not only be in place, but a mining company would, hopefully, already be on the property and setting up operations. Once that was done, it would be virtually impossible for his enemies to throw a wrench in the works.

"You're right," she agreed with a sigh. "Forget I said anything. What can I do while you're calling security?"

Thirty minutes later, David was ready to go. He'd loaded a tent and sleeping bag into the truck, insisting that Rainey and Buck use the camper for now. With Buck in the lead with the bulldozer, Rainey at his side in the pickup, and David following in the fuel truck, they turned north as they left the ranch and headed for the national forest.

Constantly checking his mirrors and the road in front of them, all Buck's attention was focused on getting the convoy safely to the ranch's back entrance. He hadn't said anything to Rainey, but he wasn't comfortable with the fact that they had to move ranch equipment on public roads. Granted, there were dozens of reasons why a ranch the size of the Broken Arrow would be using a bulldozer. Most of the local ranchers would probably pass their little convoy without thinking twice about it…unless they realized how late it was in the day and that there was normally little use for a bulldozer in the ranch's rugged northwest section. If they started thinking about the ranch's history, however, and wondering why Buck was digging anything in that area of the ranch, they might put two and two together and come up with answers he didn't want them to even think about.

When a red SUV suddenly came around a curve in front of them and passed them going the opposite direction, he tensed, only to release a silent breath when he saw that the driver was a little white-haired woman who was hardly tall enough to see over the steering wheel. As she passed, all her attention was focused on staying in her lane. Buck doubted that she even saw them.

"You're worried about someone seeing us, aren't you?"

Rainey's quiet question shattered the tense silence that filled the cab of the truck. Never taking his eyes from the road, Buck didn't deny it. "Given my druthers, I would have preferred to do this in the middle of the night, when we had less chance of being observed, but getting the bulldozer through the trees and rocks is going to be difficult enough in the light of day. I can't imagine trying such a stunt in total darkness."

"How much farther to the cutoff to the ranch?"

"Twenty kilometers," he said grimly. "Right now, it seems like a hundred."

Rainey had to agree. She found herself checking the side mirrors also, just in case they were being followed. But David brought up the rear in the gasoline truck, and there wasn't a soul behind him for as far as she could see.

She should have been relieved, but all she could think of was the driver of the black pickup who had tried to drive them off the road last week. What if he was still out there somewhere, cruising the roads that surrounded the ranch, looking for Buck? And then there was the coward who'd called her at the motel and threatened her. Was he still watching her? Did he drive a black pickup?

In her line of work, Rainey came up against desperate people all the time who would go to any lengths to get what they wanted. But in those instances, she usually knew who her enemy was. Buck didn't have a clue, and that, in itself, was terrifying. For all they knew, the little old lady they'd just passed *was* the enemy, or at least part of a larger group and was, even now, on her cell phone, reporting their activity to someone else. Buck could be driving them all right into an ambush.

"Who do you think is after the ranch?" she asked as he carefully maneuvered the camper and bulldozer through a series of S curves. "Obviously, it's someone who thinks Hilda wanted them to inherit if you couldn't meet the conditions of the will, but who is it? A neighbor? An old friend? What kind of friends did she have if they're willing to run you off the road and practically kill you to get their hands on the place?"

He didn't take his eyes from the road, but for the first time in what seemed like hours, he smiled. "I've asked myself the same thing hundreds of time, and I'm not any closer to an answer now than I was the first time someone let the air out of my truck tires when I went to town."

"Someone let the air out of your tires? Are you kidding?"

"I didn't know if it was a harmless teenage joke or something more threatening, so I called the police. Not that it did much good," he added with a grimace. "There were at least a half-dozen witnesses who had to have seen whoever did it, but they claimed they didn't know anything about the incident. That's when I knew the natives weren't going to be friendly. It's only gotten worse since then."

"In what way?"

He shrugged. "You name it, someone——or several people—have gone out of their way to let me know I'm not wanted here. First it was little things—phone calls at three in the morning even though I have an unlisted number and I've changed it four times, mail stolen out of the mailbox, which is, by the way, a federal offense—stuff like that. Then it got ugly."

"Ugly…how?"

"Someone called one of my sisters in London and told her I'd been killed in a car accident."

"Oh my God!"

"Then a dead coyote was tied to the front gate with a bloody knife stuck in it. You don't want to know about the rest."

Horrified, Rainey said, "Surely the authorities can do something."

"Yeah, right." He laughed, not the least bit amused. "The sheriff's increased patrols around the ranch, and the police have assured me they're here to protect me if anything happens in town. From what I've seen, all they do is hang out at the Rusty Bucket and drink coffee all day."

He was bitter, and Rainey couldn't blame him. "Is the ranch worth it?" she asked curiously. "Considering everything that's happened, most people wouldn't blame you if you just said to hell with it and went back to London. Of course, it's an incredibly valuable piece of property, especially if you find the mine, but is it worth living in terror for a year?"

When he hesitated, she added quickly, "Not that it's any of my business. It's your inheritance—"

"That's the kicker," he said. "If it was just a piece of land I'd bought as an investment, I'd probably sell it in a heartbeat—nothing is worth this kind of headache. The problem is, it's not an investment. My ancestors fought and died here. How can I just walk away? My sisters and I are the last of the Wyatts. I grew up reading about the Broken Arrow. Its history is in my blood. No one is driving me off it."

His jaw set at a determined angle, he turned onto the narrow lane that led to the ranch's back entrance; it took all his concentration to just to get through the trees. Behind him, David followed. Forced to cut his speed to a virtual crawl, it was, Buck realized, going to be a long, slow drive to the mine, but he didn't care. They were once again on the ranch and they'd locked the gate behind them. They were safe.

Chapter 12

Later, Rainey never knew how they got the bulldozer through the trees and boulders that turned the far northwest corner of the ranch into an obstacle course, but Buck found a way. It was, however, well after dark when they reached the canyon and set up camp. Rainey expected Buck to unload the bulldozer and start excavating as soon as the lights were set up, but the drive took longer than exptected and everyone was tired. Disappointed, Buck decided to wait until morning. By the time the sun first peeked over the horizon, David had the bulldozer warming up and ready to go. At a signal from Buck, he broke ground. The hunt for gold was on.

They quickly discovered they had their work cut out

for them. Trees had to be cut and cleared away and boulders as big as cars pushed out of the way. To make matters worse, they didn't know exactly where to dig, in spite of the fact that, according to documentation, the mine was supposedly located directly across from the bell. But was the bell in the original spot where the Spaniards had hung it or had it somehow ended up there after the avalanche? At this point, there was no way to know, so they started excavating straight across from the bell, then fanned out, steadily working their way across the canyon.

Watching them, helping as much as she could, Rainey found herself thinking of the curse and waiting for something to happen. She didn't have long to wait. Less than an hour after Buck started cutting up the tree that David had pushed out of the way with the bulldozer, the chain on the chain saw he was using snapped.

"Watch out!"

Lightning quick, he jumped out of the way, and the chain missed him by a hairbreadth.

Horrified, Rainey rushed over to him as David brought the bulldozer to a grinding halt. "Are you all right?"

He nodded grimly. "That was a little too close for comfort."

Joining them, David studied the chain, which had landed a few feet away. "I just put that chain on the week before I left—it shouldn't have done that. In fact, I've never had one do that before. Was it loose?"

"No. I tested it before I started using it. It seemed fine."

"Is there a possibility there's something wrong with the saw?" Rainey asked.

"There shouldn't be," David replied. "It was probably just a defective chain. We brought plenty of chains with us, so I'll just put a new one on."

Excusing himself, he returned to work and never saw the pointed look Rainey exchanged with Buck. "Don't go there," he warned. "This has nothing to do with the curse. You heard him. The chain was probably defective."

"Maybe," she agreed. "But he also said he'd never had one do that before, either."

"There's no curse, Rainey. It's just man-made problems and coincidence."

She hoped he was right, and for a while, it looked as if he might be. Nothing went wrong and they continued to make steady progress. Then, just when they broke for lunch, David stepped down from the bulldozer…and right into a hole. Surprised, he lost his balance and twisted his ankle.

Frowning in concern, Buck hurried to his side. "Are you all right?"

Grunting, he took a hesitant step, tested his weight on his ankle and swore. "Yeah," he grumbled. "I guess so. I feel like a damn fool. I know better than to take a step without watching where I put my feet."

"Accidents happen," Buck said. Shooting Rainey a warning look before she could bring up the curse, he added, "Just be careful, okay? We're a long way from a hospital."

"Are you sure you're all right?" Rainey asked the older man in concern. "Maybe you should see a doctor—"

"Oh, no, ma'am!" he said quickly, shocked. "I don't want anything to do with doctors. I'll be fine."

"If you change your mind, just let us know," Buck told him. "Let's break for lunch. I think we can all use it."

The afternoon and evening came and went, and there was still no sign of the mine. Rainey knew the odds of finding it quickly were slim, but she still couldn't help but be disappointed.

"We're making progress," Buck assured her and David as they called it a day. "Tomorrow will be better."

But they spent the next three days digging, combing through the rock and dirt for the mine, and they still had nothing to show for all their effort. The security Buck had hired arrived on Monday, but there was nothing to guard.

Still, Rainey refused to give up hope. "It's here," she told Buck as they watched David move the bulldozer slightly west of where they had been working. "It has to be here somewhere. We found the bell, the creek. Even the curse is working!"

"There you go again, being superstitious," Buck said, chuckling. "Accidents happen. They have nothing to do with a curse."

The words were hardly out of his mouth when David

attempted to roll over a boulder in the bulldozer as he started up a small rocky hill. Without warning, the ground beneath it gave way, and the bulldozer lurched roughly to the right, throwing David out of the driver's seat.

"What the hell!"

"Oh my God! Is he hurt?"

Buck and Rainey ran to his assistance, as did the two security guards, but David was already on his feet and dusting himself off by the time they reached him. "I'm okay," he said before anyone could ask. "I don't know what happened…son of a gun! Look at that!"

The entire group followed his gaze to where the bull-dozer's shovel had dug into the side of the hill when it lurched sideways. The force of the accident had moved two large boulders and sent them rolling down the hill. And there, in the place where they had, no doubt, lain for centuries, was a hole that looked like the opening of a cave…or a mine.

Her knees suddenly turning to rubber, Rainey reached blindly for Buck. "Is that—"

"It damn sure is!" Buck laughed, and pulled her into his arms for a fierce kiss. "What do you think of your curse now?"

Later, Rainey never remembered the drive back to the house. She and Buck laughed and talked and the miles magically flew by. As soon as they reached the house, he had to call the mining companies he'd already re-searched and begin negotiations with them to operate the mine. In the meantime, David stayed behind to continue working the bulldozer while the security guards patrolled the canyon and mine entrances.

Still unable to believe how everything had come together, Rainey could hardly sit still. "Do you know how much of this was just pure chance? When I was doing research in Spain, I never intended to go to Barcelona, where I discovered the records of the mine in a private library."

Surprised, he said, "I thought you already knew where the records were."

"No, not at all. I was doing research at the University of Madrid library when I came across a reference to a family in seventeenth-century Barcelona whose son came to America with the first Spanish missionaries. I traced their family tree and discovered that their descendants were still living in Barcelona on the land the family had owned for over three hundred years. Can you believe that? What are the odds that they hadn't sold out to developers years ago? Or died out? I went to visit them, they gave me access to their family library, and I never went anywhere else."

"You're kidding!"

"And then there's the bell," she reminded him. "If I hadn't fallen down that hill, we would have probably never found it. Think about it. You own thousands of acres that match the seventeenth-century description of the mine's location. We could have spent the next ten years hiking through every canyon on the ranch and never found it."

"You won't get an argument out of me," he told her as they left the ranch's back entrance and reached the county road that led to the ranch's main entrance. "I still can't believe how David found the mine. Or maybe I should say, how the bulldozer did. Talk about a freak accident. I really thought David had been hurt. Then the next thing I know, there's the mine, right in front of us!"

"It was fate," she said happily, "just like the bell. I know you don't believe in it, but some things are just meant to be. Regardless of what you do, you can't screw it up."

"I never said I didn't believe in fate," he said as he turned into the ranch's main entrance and then the circular driveway in front of the house. "There's no question that there are forces at work in the world other than our own. Speaking of which, since fate has thrown you—and the gold mine—in my path, I think we should celebrate tonight. I'll take you out to dinner. We'll go dancing."

Delighted, Rainey immediately thought of her limited wardrobe. "Make it country-western dancing and you've got a deal," she said as he parked and they both stepped from the truck. "All I brought with me was jeans. Have you ever line danced?"

Unlocking the front door, he grinned. "No, but I'm sure you can teach—"

When he broke off abruptly at the sight of a taxi turning into the driveway, Rainey turned to follow his gaze and gasped in surprise. "Who would be crazy enough to take a taxi all the way out here?"

"I don't know," he murmured. "I'm not expecting anyone." Frowning, he watched as the taxi pulled behind his truck and the driver came around and opened the back door for the passenger. At the sight of the woman stepping from the taxi, Buck blinked. "My God!"

"What is it?" Rainey asked. "Who is she?"

"Melissa."

That was all he said, just her name, but that was all it took for Rainey's heart to drop. Melissa. His former fiancée. The woman he loved. The woman who'd refused to move to Colorado with him. Obviously, she'd changed her mind.

The tall, leggy blonde spied him then and rushed forward with her arms outstretched. "Darling!" When he just looked at her, stunned, she hesitated. "Didn't you get my letter?"

"What letter?"

"The one I sent saying I'd made a terrible mistake, that I still loved you and wanted to make up. I told you I had a wedding to attend in New York, and I wanted to see you while I was in the States. If you didn't want to see me, you were supposed to e-mail me telling me that. You didn't so I assumed…"

"I never got your letter," he said flatly.

"It doesn't matter—I'm here now, and I love you. You have to know I wouldn't chance coming here, facing you, if I didn't love you. Forgive me?"

"Melissa—"

"God, how I've missed the sound of my name on

your lips!" And with no other warning than that, she threw herself into his arms and kissed him.

For the first time in his life, he was speechless. *He didn't love her anymore.* He didn't know how or when it had happened, but the second she kissed him as if there had never been a cross word between them, he knew whatever feelings he'd once had for her were colder than a North Sea herring.

If his mother hadn't raised him to be a gentleman, he would have told her right then and there, but that wasn't a conversation he could have with her in front of Rainey. Regardless of how he felt about her now, she was the woman he had once asked to be his wife, and he couldn't be that cruel.

Pulling back abruptly, he said, "We need to talk."

"Of course, darling." She laughed, linking her arm through his and hugging him close. "First, you need to introduce me to your friend." Holding out her hand to Rainey, she smiled coolly. "Hello, I'm Melissa Gibson, Buck's fiancée. And you are…?"

"Rainey Brewster," she said just as coolly. The last thing she wanted to do was shake Melissa's hand, but she hadn't missed the challenge in her eye. Without hesitation, she took her hand. "I'm a business associate of Buck's. Obviously, you two must have a lot to talk about, so I'll get out of your way. It was nice to meet you."

Her eyes burned with the threat of tears, but she held them off with a smile that didn't waver and forced herself to face Buck. It wasn't easy. She felt as though he'd ripped her heart to shreds and he hadn't even touched her. He hadn't had to. All he had to do was kiss another woman.

"I imagine you'd like to show Melissa the ranch," she said quietly. "I'll be in my room catching up on my e-mails." Without another word, she turned and hurried inside.

"Rainey, wait—"

"Yes, darling, I'd love to see the ranch," Melissa purred, tugging him back to her side when he would have pulled away. "I can't wait to see everything." Kissing his ear, she murmured, "It's been a long time, Buck. Too long. Pay the cabbie, darling, and take me somewhere we can be alone. Let me show you how much I've missed you."

Hardly hearing her, Buck swore silently. He could just imagine what Rainey thought when Melissa had thrown herself in his arms. He had to go after her, had to explain. But first, he had to deal with Melissa.

Abruptly putting her from him, he ignored her murmur of protest and turned to the taxi driver, who was busily pulling Melissa's luggage from the boot of the cab. There were already six cases sitting next to the car, and he was pulling out more.

"I hate to do this to you, old man," he told the cabbie, "but you need to put all that right back in the boot. The lady's not staying."

For a moment, there was nothing but stunned silence. Then Melissa gasped. "What? Darling, you can't be serious! I just got here."

"You weren't invited, *darling,*" he retorted, then turned his attention back to the cabbie, who was re-loading Melissa's cases back in the boot piece by piece. "Thank you, sir. I'll pay you, of course, for every piece. If you'll excuse us for a moment, the lady and I need to talk."

"Take your time," he said cheerfully. "The meter's running."

"Dammit, Buck!" Melissa cried as he took her arm and escorted her inside to his office. "You can't do this! What's wrong with you?"

"You made it very clear that you wanted nothing to do with Colorado or me if I insisted on living here," he patiently reminded her. "You're the one who broke our engagement, not me."

"You caught me off guard. You know I don't handle surprises well. I have to think about it."

"For four months?"

"You were asking me to change all my plans for the future, to leave England, for heaven's sake! I had to think about it, come to terms with it. And I did! Because I love you. I didn't realize how much until you were gone."

There was a time when he would have given just about anything to hear her say that, but not anymore. "I took you at your word, Melissa," he said quietly. "I've moved on."

Confused, she frowned. "Moved on? What are you saying? You've found someone else?" The truth hit her then, and she laughed. "Are you talking about that mousy little brunette who just scurried up to her room? Your *business associate?* Nice try, sweetheart, but I know you. You may be sleeping with her but you're not in love with her. She's not nearly sophisticated enough for you."

His jaw clenched on an oath. Buck had no intention of discussing Rainey or his feelings for her with Melissa. "You weren't invited here," he said coldly. "If you'd bothered to call first—"

"*I wrote you a letter!*"

"I would have told you not to come," he continued. "I'm sorry, but you have to leave."

"Dammit Buck—"

"The cabbie's waiting," he said stiffly. "Come on, I'll walk you out."

If looks could kill, he would have dropped dead right then and there. "If you humiliate me this way, I'll never forgive you," she said coldly. "Your name will be mud in England."

Unconcerned, he smiled mockingly. "It may be, but at least yours will never be Wyatt. Now if you'll excuse me, I have better things to do." Without a word, he turned and walked into the house.

Left standing alone on the front drive, she had no choice but to climb into the taxi and head back to the airport.

The hot water from the shower raining down on her, Rainey stood with her head bent, hugging herself as tears squeezed through her tightly closed eyelids. When she'd reached her room—she'd walked straight to the bathroom and stepped into the shower, clothes and all. Still chilled, all she'd wanted was for the hurt to go away. The pain squeezing her heart, however, went bone deep. It would, she knew, be a long time—if ever— before she stopped hurting.

He was still in love with Melissa.

Numb, she still couldn't believe it. The woman was a witch! What in the world did he see in her? Okay, so she was beautiful. She didn't love him, Rainey didn't care what Melissa said. If she had, she would have never let him come to Colorado without her. She would have—

Suddenly realizing what she was doing, she swore softly. It didn't matter if Melissa loved Buck. The only thing that mattered was that he loved her.

She couldn't stay here.

The realization stabbed her right in the heart, but there was no denying it. Oh, she wasn't leaving Colorado and walking away from the treasure she'd been searching for for years—that would be insane. They had a contract, and by God, she was going to stick around to make sure that it was honored. Once the mine was up and running and she didn't need to stay to protect her investment, she didn't think she would ever step foot in Colorado again.

In the meantime, she couldn't continue to stay at the Broken Arrow, not now that he and Melissa had made up. It just hurt too much. She'd go back to the motel in town. Today.

Just stay one more night, her heart pleaded. *Don't run*

away just because that *woman showed up. Talk to him, remind him what the two of you shared.*

Tempted, she would have given anything to be that much of a masochist, but she couldn't. She refused to be one of those sad, clingy, pathetic women who couldn't let go. It was over. That meant she had to move out—immediately.

The decision made, she pulled off her wet clothes and took a quick shower. Twenty minutes later, she was packed and ready to go. Refusing to shed so much as a single tear, she grabbed her suitcase and headed downstairs before she could change her mind.

Buck was, no doubt, out showing Melissa around. She might be taking the coward's way out by leaving without speaking to him, but she wanted to spare them both what could only be an awkward moment. She'd written a note to leave on his desk—when he read it, he would, hopefully, understand why she left the way she had.

Anxious to be gone, she rushed into his office and was nearly to his desk when she realized she wasn't alone. Buck stood at the window, looking out at the front driveway. At her nearly soundless gasp, he turned and their eyes met.

She wanted to cry, to demand to know how he could make love with her when he was in love with someone else, but she couldn't. Instead, pride lifted her chin, and she heard herself say, "I'm sorry. I thought you went to show Melissa around the ranch. I was just leaving you a note, though I guess I don't need to do that now. I'm moving back into town, Buck."

His eyes narrowed, searching hers. "That's not necessary."

"Oh, yes, it is," she retorted. "As much as I've enjoyed our time together, we both always knew it couldn't last. You know how I hate the idea of being tied down. Lately I've been getting itchy feet and thinking about the next job. As soon as the mine is up and running, I'll be leaving anyway. This is a good time to get back on the right track."

Stunned, Buck felt as if she'd just kicked him in the gut. "You don't think we need to talk about this?"

"There's nothing to talk about," she said firmly. "We're business partners, nothing more. I just need you to pay me the finder's fee we agreed on, and then when the mine is in operation, I'm on my way to Virginia. There's a woman in Richmond who wants me to help her find the family jewels that were buried in a cemetery during the Civil War."

Every instinct Buck had warned him not to let her go. They had to talk—he had to tell her he loved her. Then, if she still wanted to leave, so be it. But she was so cool and professional, and he couldn't forget the fact that she had never given any indication that she had any feelings for him other than like and lust. Even as his heart was screaming at him to tell her how he felt about her, his pride refused to let him ask her to stay.

"I believe the finder's fee was a twenty-five-hundred-dollar advance when the mine was found, then a ten-thousand-dollar payment when the mine was operational."

"And a twelve percent royalty against the gross for the next ten years," she added.

"Plus a twelve percent royalty," he repeated as he strode over to his desk and sat down to write a check for her. Holding it out to her, his eyes met hers. "I presume when you leave, you'll want your checks sent to the address in your contract?"

She nodded stiffly. "Thank you."

Folding the check, she slipped it into the pocket of her jeans, then hesitated. For a moment, Buck thought she was going to offer her hand just like any other business partner at the completion of a deal, but then she obviously thought better of it and stepped back.

"Well, I have to go," she said quietly. "I'll see you tomorrow at the mine."

Without another word, she turned and walked out.

Later, Rainey never knew how she found her car, let alone drove away. She should have headed for town, then for Virginia, just like she'd said she was, but as she reached the end of the driveway, she knew she couldn't. Not yet.

She turned right instead of left and headed toward the national forest and the back entrance to the ranch. Searching for the mine with Buck was an experience she knew she would never forget, and as she reached the national forest and approached the dirt path that led to the gate to the ranch, memories flooded through her. Without even closing her eyes, she could see Buck that first day, when he'd shut the door in her face, then again, when he'd kissed her for the first time…and made love to her. And once again, tears welled in her eyes and spilled over her lashes.

Later, she never knew how she made it to the canyon without hitting something. Her eyes hurt, her vision was blurred, and every time she thought of Buck, fresh tears once again made it impossible for her to see. Her angels must have been leading her. She didn't so much as even scrape a tree.

Then, suddenly, the canyon was right in front of her, and all she could think of was Buck as she parked and headed for the mine on foot. He should have been there, she thought, savoring the discovery of the mine, not entertaining a woman who'd never supported his dream of living on the ranch to begin with. He needed someone who would love the ranch and its heritage as much as he did. Someone who would—

Her eyes on the rough terrain and where she was putting her feet, she stopped to check how far she was from the mine when she suddenly realized the place was deserted. Surprised, she frowned. Where was David? And the security guards? When she and Buck left earlier, David had been busily working at the mine entrance, digging away more dirt and making sure it was safe. The security guards had taken up positions close to the canyon entrance and set up a security check. So where were they?

Concerned, she hurried through the trees toward the

mine. Surely they hadn't gone inside. It was too danger-ous. No one had been in there for over two hundred years, and there was a good possibility that the avalanche had weakened the support beams. If there was a cave-in…

Blanching at the thought, she was still a hundred feet from the mine entrance when a movement out of the corner of her eye caught her attention and she turned to see David walk out from behind a large boulder not far from the mine entrance. Relieved, she started forward, smiling. "There you are," she began. "I—"

Her eyes dropped to the roll of wire and the detona-tor he set on the ground, and whatever she was going to say next flew right out of her head. She wasn't an ex-plosives expert by any means, but she'd seen dynamite used enough times over the course of the years to rec-ognize a pending explosion when she saw one. "What are you doing? You can't…"

"I can do any damn thing I want," he snapped, and jerked a small pistol out of his pocket. Before she could so much as blink, he aimed it right at her heart. "Don't even think about stopping me."

Heart pounding, she didn't move so much as a muscle. "Why are you doing this?"

"Why do you think? Money, of course."

"But Buck is on the verge of making a fortune! He's not a tightfisted man. He'll pay you fair wages."

"Somebody else is paying me more," he retorted. "A hell of a lot more!"

"To destroy the mine?"

He nodded grimly. "I tried to stop Buck from finding it—if he didn't have any money to run the place, he'd have to go home—but he didn't pay any attention."

"*You* rigged those accidents? You couldn't have. You were gone. Your mother—"

"Died years ago," he said smugly. "I've been here the whole time."

"What? Why?"

"I had to convince Buck that the Indian curse was true so he'd back off and leave the mine alone. But it didn't work, so now I'm going to blow the thing to kingdom come and kill a few people in the process. If that doesn't convince him he's not wanted here, nothing will."

She blanched. "*Kill a few people?* Where are the security guards?"

He didn't so much as blink. "In the mine. Buck did me a favor when he had one of them guard the mine entrance and the other the entrance to the canyon. All I had to do was sneak up on each of them and knock them out. And now it's your turn to join them."

Her heart in her throat, Rainey knew if she made the mistake of letting him force her into the mine, she would never come out alive. If she was going to die, then she would do it here, outside in the open, where she could take her chances.

"C'mon," he growled, motioning her toward the mine with the pistol. "Move it."

Her mind working furiously, she had no choice but to start towards the mine entrance. "You're not going to get away with this."

"Shut up!"

"What are you going to do? Kill all three of us? Everyone's going to know you did it. You'll be the only one left standing."

"I told you to *shut up!*"

"Buck will come after you—"

"No!"

Enraged, he grabbed her arm, just as she hoped he would. When he jerked her around to face him, she was ready. With a fierce cry, she launched herself at him, clawing at his eyes.

"Aaagh! You bitch! Whore—" Curses streaming off his tongue, he swung wildly at her and caught her on the jaw. She went flying...so did the gun.

Sobbing, her jaw throbbing and her eyes watering from the pain, she sprang up, scrambling for the gun. David got there first.

Twenty minutes after Rainey left, Buck took the now familiar path to the mine to help David with the excavation of the mines entrance. He'd put the call into the mining company, but he'd forgotten it was Saturday, and all he'd gotten was the company answering machine. He'd left a message, but doubted anyone would be in until Monday to return his call.

The second he'd hung up the phone, all he could

think about was Rainey. He should have told her he loved her. He was thirty-two years old and had finally found the woman he knew was right for him, and he'd let her leave without telling her how he felt about her. What the devil was wrong with him? Was he afraid she'd reject him? Tell him she didn't love him?

Like hell! He'd held the woman, kissed her, made love to her. He knew when a woman loved him, and there wasn't a doubt in his mind that Rainey had feelings for him. But she'd left without a backward glance. Why? How could she if she really loved him?

How would you feel if you'd caught her kissing her ex-husband? Would you think she loved you if she was kissing someone she'd once loved and had a history with?

He wasn't kissing Melissa, he told himself. But he could understand how Rainey might have been too upset to notice that little distinction.

As he approached the entrance to the canyon where the mine was located, he wondered what the hell he was doing there. He should have followed Rainey, all the way to Virginia if he had to, and told her he loved her. Then if she was still determined to keep their relationship strictly business, that was her choice, but at least she'd be dealing with all the facts.

Cursing himself for an idiot, he started to turn around, only to hit the brakes at the sight of Rainey's car parked under a tree just inside the canyon. *She was here?*

Quickly parking behind her, he cut the engine and headed through the trees to where the mine was located halfway down the length of the canyon. He was still fifty yards away when he heard David yell, "You bitch! Whore!"

What the hell? At the sound of Rainey's scream, Buck broke into a run and burst through the trees just in time to see David slap Rainey to the ground, then beat her to the gun that had just been knocked free. "You son of a bitch!" Buck snarled, and launched himself at his foreman.

David had no time to do anything but turn before Buck tackled him, driving him into the ground. Somewhere over the hot fury roaring in his ears, Buck thought he heard Rainey scream something at him, but he couldn't understand her. Then David slammed his fist into his mouth, knocking him aside, and he scrambled to his feet just in time to see Rainey snatch up the gun that David had once again dropped in the scuffle. "Freeze!" Rainey cried. "I mean it. I'll shoot!"

Far from intimidated, David grabbed a rock and turned on her, throwing it at her head. Horrified, Rainey pulled the trigger.

The bullet whizzed past David's ear, so close he had to feel the heat. Swearing, he stepped back…and stumbled over the dynamite detonator.

Muttering an oath, he caught himself, but not before he pushed the plunger nearly all the way down. For what seemed like an eternity, nobody moved. Then he turned with a look of pure horror on his face. "Run!"

Buck grabbed Rainey and pulled her after him, but he'd only taken two steps when a rumble deep in the depths of the mine shook the ground beneath their feet. That was the only warning they got. A split second later, the mine exploded, and all hell broke loose.

Rainey screamed—she must have, though later she had no memory of it—as rocks and dirt rained from the sky. Clods of dirt pounded her head and shoulders, and next to her, Buck grunted as a broken tree limb glanced off his shoulder. "The trees," he grunted, his shoulder bumping hers as he tried to steer her away from the open area in front of the mine. "We'll be safer in the trees."

Running deep into a thick stand of pines, Rainey was gasping for air when she tripped on a root and went down hard. Surprised, Buck ran past her before he realized she was down. Rushing back to her side, he snatched her to her feet. "All you all right? What happened?"

"I tripped," she said hoarsely, dragging in a deep breath. "David—"

Buck looked back behind then, only to swear. "Stay here. He's hurt."

"Be careful!" she called after him.

The words were hardly out of her mouth when he returned to her side, his expression grim. "What's wrong?" she asked, frowning. "Is he all right?"

He hesitated, then admitted quietly, "His skull was crushed by a rock, love. He's dead."

What little color remained in her cheeks vanished. "Oh my God!"

"Where are the security guards? Weren't they here when you got here?"

Suddenly remembering, she looked at him in horror, instant tears flooding her eyes. "They were in the mine! Oh my God, I killed them!"

"No, you didn't," he said fiercely, reaching for her. "You didn't do anything but defend yourself."

"But David would have never fallen if it hadn't been for me," she argued, stricken. "I didn't think, didn't realize—"

"Stop!" he told her firmly, hugging her tight. "In case you've forgotten, love, the bastard was trying to kill both of us. You saved *our* lives, so stop beating yourself up. Tell me about the guards. How do you know they were in the mine? Did you see them?"

"No, but David said—"

"Stop and think about it, sweetheart. It was two against one, and they both had guns. Do you really think two armed men would have meekly let David force them into the mine without a fight?"

"Well, no," she replied, wiping the tears from her cheeks. "Not when you put it that way. So where are they?"

"They could still be dead," he warned her. "But I'll bet you your finder's fee that they're not in the mine. C'mon, let's look for them."

Latching on to his hand, she wasn't about to let him out of her sight. "Wait! We need to call the sheriff—"

"The cell phones won't pick up from here," he reminded her. "We'll have to wait until we get back to the house to call."

Together, they moved into the trees at the edge of the

clearing, looking for some sign of what happened to the two missing men. "What the hell went on here after we left?" Buck asked as their search led them in an ever-widening circle around the mine. "Why would David dynamite the mine?"

"Someone paid him to drive you away from the ranch," she replied as tears once again welled in her eyes. "I couldn't get him to tell me who, though, and now we'll never know."

"Yes, we will," he promised her grimly. "Whoever he was working for isn't going to stop trying to drive me away just because David died. He'll find someone else to do his dirty work, and sooner or later, he's going to give himself away."

Rainey knew he was right, but that didn't make her feel any better. "I know, but—" Suddenly stiffening, she frowned. "Did you hear that?"

Tugged to a stop beside her, he cocked his head. "What? Wait! Over there! See—behind those boulders to the right—that looks like—"

"The security guards! Thank God!"

The sheriff, an ambulance and the county coroner all arrived at the Broken Arrow within minutes of each other and had to follow Buck and Rainey to the mine and explosion site. There was no question that David had died from a blow to the head during the explosion, but there was little sympathy expressed for him by the two men he'd knocked out one by one, then tied up.

They both had concussions and were furious with themselves for being so easily duped by the man.

"Are you kidding?" Buck said when they tried to apologize to him. "This isn't your fault. I'm the one who hired him. I even had him checked out."

"And you didn't find anything out of the ordinary?" Sheriff Clark asked with a frown.

"No, nothing. Oh, he'd been out of work due to an injury he suffered in a car wreck and he had a few credit problems he was trying to work out, but that didn't seem all that serious. I never dreamed he was taking bribes from my enemies."

Glancing up from the notes he was taking, Sherm Clark shot him a sharp look. "Any idea who these enemies are? Who did he hang out with?"

"No one that I know of," he admitted. "I never saw him with anyone. The only person I ever heard him talk about was his mother. He told me she was dying, that he was her only living relative and needed time off to take care of her, but apparently, that was all a lie. He told Rainey his mother died years ago, and he was skulking around the ranch the entire time he was supposedly gone."

"Do you think that's true?"

He shrugged. "At this point, I don't know what to think."

"I'll check it out," he promised. "In the meantime, what do you plan to do about the mine?"

"It's blown to hell," he retorted. "David's dead and the four of us could have been killed in the explosion.

At this point, I think I'm going to let it go, at least until the trial period is up for the ranch."

"Oh, no, Buck!" Rainey cried. "You can't do that!"

"I'm not going to take a chance on anyone else getting killed," he told her flatly. "Especially you. The mine's been here for two hundred years. Now that we know its exact location, we can excavate it whenever we like."

"He's right," Sherm told Rainey soberly. "It's not going anywhere. And in the meantime, I'll see what I can find out about David. If he was taking bribes from someone in the area, someone's bound to know about it. Sooner or later, it's going to come out."

"Thank you, Sheriff," Buck said, shaking his hand. "I can use all the help you can give me."

"I'll do what I can," he promised. "The coroner's already removed the body, and these two—" he nodded toward the security guards "—insist they don't need to go to the hospital. What about you two? You've got more than a few scrapes and bruises. If you want the paramedics to take a look at you, speak now—"

"We're fine," Buck assured him. "Thanks, anyway."

"No problem," he said easily. "Call if anything else happens."

The paramedics carefully followed him out of the canyon and soon disappeared from view. "We'll be taking off, too," the older of the two security guards told Buck, offering his hand. "If you decide to reopen the mine, let us know."

"That's right," the other man said. "We hate getting beat by the bad guys. Next time, we won't be caught off guard."

"I don't know if there's going to be a next time," Buck said honestly, "but I appreciate the offer. Thanks."

They headed for their car, and seconds later, everyone was gone…except Rainey. Buck wanted to reach for her, to reassure himself he hadn't lost her, but first he had to clear the air. "I'm not back with Melissa," he said quietly. "I sent her back to town. She's going to London on the first available flight."

Whatever Rainey had been expecting him to say, it wasn't that. Stunned, she looked up at him searchingly. "You kissed her. I thought—"

"No, *she* kissed me," he corrected her, "not the other way around. And I know what you thought. I don't blame you. I would have thought the same thing if the situation had been reversed.

"I don't love her anymore," he said. "I already knew that, but seeing her again verified it. I would have told her right then, but telling the old love in front of the new love that I didn't love her anymore seemed kind of crass."

Startled, her heart pounding, Rainey desperately wanted to believe she'd heard him correctly, but like him, she needed verification. "Did you say *new love?* I would have sworn that's what you said, but sometimes my ears have been known to play tricks on me. And I don't want to be accused of hearing what I want to hear—"

Grinning, he reached for her. "You know, I do believe I did say *new love*. Do you have a problem with that?"

Joy sparkling in her eyes, she pretended to consider. "Well, let's see. You do have this wonderful accent—"

"No, darling, that's you."

"And you're a fantastic kisser—"

"Sweetheart, you have to stop talking about yourself. We're talking about me, remember?"

"Oh, yes," she chuckled. "I beg your pardon. Okay, let me think." She looped her arms around his neck. I don't know what to say. You're just so lovable—"

"There you go again," he sighed, fighting a grin. "It's always about you."

Rainey could think of a dozen things she could have said to keep the teasing game going, but only one mattered. Sudden tears flooding her eyes, she softly, gently, pressed her mouth to his. "I love you," she whispered. "I didn't think I'd ever see you again."

"I was never going to let that happen, love," he said. "I realized when I came here to the mine that I was going to go after you. I just came here first to help David with the excavation, I knew you needed some time."

"I was devastated."

"I don't want you to ever leave," he told her. "Marry me. I'm not your ex," he added quickly, before she could say anything. "I don't expect you to walk away from a career you love to help me get this ranch back on its feet. But the mine would have never been found without you. You should be here to help excavate it, work it—we can do it together."

"That would be wonderful, but—"

"We need to wait until we have a clear title, though. It's just too dangerous, otherwise."

"I agree, but—"

"And you don't have to worry about being tied to the ranch until the year is up," he added. "We can go anywhere you like, go do research, look for treasure— I just have to get one of my sisters to take over for me."

"I would love that, but I—"

"You might even find something on the ranch—"

She stopped him with a kiss. Then another. When she finally let him up for air, he grinned at her crookedly. "What was that for?"

"If you'd stop talking, I might be able to get a word in edgewise."

His grin faded. This was it. One word. She only needed one. Yes? No? Maybe? Wincing at the thought— she couldn't do that to him—he sighed, bracing himself. "Okay, take your shot. What's the word?"

To her credit, she didn't drag out the torture. Her eyes met his, her fingers linked with his, and he started to grin before she ever opened her mouth. "Yes."

Epilogue

Rainey was in the library reading Buck's great-grand-father's journal, when Buck found her stretched out on the couch, totally engrossed. Leaning over the back of the couch, he snatched the book out of her hands before she knew he was there and kissed her fiercely.

"Buck!"

"*Rainey!*" he teased.

"Who was that on the phone?" she asked.

"The sheriff."

Her heart racing, she sat up straighter. "Did he find out anything about David?"

He nodded. "He checked the info I gave him on David and none of it was correct, not even his name. Unless his fingerprints pop up in some law enforcement's database, we'll probably never know who he really was."

"What about the man who hired him to sabotage you and the ranch? Was he able to discover anything about him?"

"Not yet," he said. "He's not holding out much hope, so it looks like life continues as usual. We still don't know who we can trust, so we don't trust anyone."

Glancing at the book she'd snatched back from him, he smiled. "What are you reading?"

"Your great-grandfather's journal. You didn't tell me how fascinating it was. You should contact someone in Hollywood. This is a movie."

"Old Buck was quite a character. Sometimes I feel like I'm living his life in reverse."

"Do you realize he was the same age as you are now when he met your great-grandmother and they became engaged?"

"Actually, I did know that. He knew the first time he laid eyes on Lily that she was the woman for him. He spent the next three years trying to convince her they were made for each other."

She flashed her dimples at him. "I couldn't have held out for three years and you know it."

"Can you hold out until May third?"

"Hold out for what? What happens May third?"

"It's the hundredth anniversary of Buck and Lily's wedding. I thought it might be a good day to get married."

Rainey's heart stopped in her chest. "You want to get married in a month?"

He grinned. "Sweetheart, I'd do it tomorrow if I thought I could talk you into it. So what do you say? Is it a date?"

She should have said no. There was so much to do! She wanted a wedding. Nothing fancy, just something here on the ranch, with friends and family present, and the mountains in the background. She had to plan the menu, get the decorations, *find a dress!* How could she do it all in a month?

How could she not?

"The third of May, hmm?" she said, her blue eyes dancing. "I believe I can make that. What time?"

"I was thinking eight."

"In the evening?"

"In the morning."

"The morning! Buck—"

"I want to start the rest of my life with you as soon as possible. Besides," he added, "I think I still owe you a breakfast."

Laughing, she went into his arms. "Actually, you owe me dinner, but we can settle that later…in about fifty years."

* * * * *

**Every Life Has More
Than One Chapter**

Award-winning author Stevi Mittman delivers
another hysterical mystery, featuring Teddi Bayer,
an irrepressible heroine, and her to-die-for hero,
Detective Drew Scoones. After all, life on Long
Island can be murder!

*Turn the page for a sneak peek at the warm
and funny fourth book,
WHOSE NUMBER IS UP, ANYWAY?
in the Teddi Bayer series,
by STEVI MITTMAN.
On sale August 7*

"Before redecorating a room, I always advise my clients to empty it of everything but one chair. Then I suggest they move that chair from place to place, sitting in it, until the placement feels right. Trust your instincts when deciding on furniture placement. Your room should 'feel right.'"

—TipsFromTeddi.com

Gut feelings. You know, that gnawing in the pit of your stomach that warns you that you are about to do the absolute stupidest thing you could do? Something that will ruin life as you know it?

I've got one now, standing at the butcher counter in King Kullen, the grocery store in the same strip mall as L.I. Lanes, the bowling alley cum billiard parlor I'm in the process of redecorating for its "Grand Opening."

I realize being in the wrong supermarket probably doesn't sound exactly dire to you, but you aren't the one buying your father a brisket at a store your mother will somehow know isn't Waldbaum's.

And then, June Bayer isn't your mother.

The woman behind the counter has agreed to go into the freezer to find a brisket for me, since there aren't any in the case. There are packages of pork tenderloin, piles of spare ribs and rolls of sausage, but no briskets.

Warning Number Two, right? I should be so out of here.

But no, I'm still in the same spot when she comes back out, brisketless, her face ashen. She opens her mouth as if she is going to scream, but only a gurgle comes out.

And then she pinballs out from behind the counter, knocking bottles of Peter Luger Steak Sauce to the floor on her way, now hitting the tower of cans at the end of the prepared foods aisle and sending them sprawling, now making her way down the aisle, careening from side to side as she goes.

Finally, from a distance, I hear her shout, "He's deeeeeeaaaad! Joey's deeeeeaaaad."

My first thought is *You should always trust your gut.*

My second thought is that now, somehow, my mother

will know I was in King Kullen. For weeks I will have to hear "What did you expect?" as though whenever you go to King Kullen someone turns up dead. And if the detective investigating the case turns out to be Detective Drew Scoones…well, I'll never hear the end of that from her, either.

She still suspects I murdered the guy who was found dead on my doorstep last Halloween just to get Drew back into my life.

Several people head for the butcher's freezer and I position myself to block them. If there's one thing I've learned from finding people dead—and the guy on my doorstep wasn't the first one—it's that the police get very testy when you mess with their murder scenes.

"You can't go in there until the police get here," I say, stationing myself at the end of the butcher's counter and in front of the Employees Only door, acting as if I'm some sort of authority. "You'll contaminate the evidence if it turns out to be murder."

Shouts and chaos. You'd think I'd know better than to throw the word *murder* around. Cell phones are flipping open and tongues are wagging.

I amend my statement quickly. "Which, of course, it probably isn't. Murder, I mean. People die all the time, and it's not always in hospitals or their own beds, or…" I babble when I'm nervous, and the idea of someone dead on the other side of the freezer door makes me very nervous.

So does the idea of seeing Drew Scoones again.

Drew and I have this on-again, off-again sort of thing…that I kind of turned off.

Who knew he'd take it so personally when he tried to get serious and I responded by saying we could talk about *us* tomorrow—and then caught a plane to my parents' condo in Boca the next day? In July. In the middle of a job.

For some crazy reason, he took that to mean that I was avoiding him and the subject of *us*.

That was three months ago. I haven't seen him since.

The manager, who identifies himself and points to his nameplate in case I don't believe him, says he has to go into *his cooler*. "Maybe Joey's not dead," he says. "Maybe he can be saved, and you're letting him die in there. Did you ever think of that?"

In fact, I hadn't. But I had thought that the murderer might try to go back in to make sure his tracks were covered, so I say that I will go in and check.

Which means that the manager and I couple up and go in together while everyone pushes against the doorway to peer in, erasing any chance of finding clean prints on that Employee Only door.

I expect to find carcasses of dead animals hanging from hooks, and maybe Joey hanging from one, too. I think it's going to be very creepy and I steel myself, only to find a rather benign series of shelves with large slabs of meat laid out carefully on them, along with boxes and boxes marked simply Chicken.

Nothing scary here, unless you count the body of a middle-aged man with graying hair sprawled faceup on the floor. His eyes are wide open and unblinking. His shirt is stiff. His pants are stiff. His body is stiff. And his expression, you should forgive the pun—is frozen. Bill-the-manager crosses himself and stands mute while I pronounce the guy dead in a sort of *happy now?* tone.

"We should not be in here," I say, and he nods his head emphatically and helps me push people out of the doorway just in time to hear the police sirens and see the cop cars pull up outside the big store windows.

Bobbie Lyons, my partner in Teddi Bayer Interior Designs (and also my neighbor, my best friend and my private fashion police), and Mark, our carpenter (and my dogsitter, confidant and ego booster), rush in from next door. They beat the cops by a half step and shout out my name. People point in my direction.

After all the publicity that followed the unfortunate incident during which I shot my ex-husband, Rio Gallo, and then the subsequent murder of my first client— which I solved, I might add—it seems like the whole world, or at least all of Long Island, knows who I am.

Mark asks if I'm all right. (Did I remember to mention that the man is drop-dead-gorgeous-but-a-decade-too-young-for-me-yet-too-old-for-my-daughter-thank-god?) I don't get a chance to answer him because the police are quickly closing in on the store manager and me.

"The woman—" I begin telling the police. Then I have to pause for the manager to fill in her name, which he does: *Fran.*

I continue. "Right. Fran. Fran went into the freezer

to get a brisket. A moment later she came out and screamed that Joey was dead. So I'd say she was the one who discovered the body."

"And you are…?" the cop asks me. It comes out a bit like who do I *think* I am, rather than who am I really?

"An innocent bystander," Bobbie, hair perfect, makeup just right, says, carefully placing her body between the cop and me.

"And she was just leaving," Mark adds. They each take one of my arms.

Fran comes into the inner circle surrounding the cops. In case it isn't obvious from the hairnet and blood-stained white apron with *Fran* embroidered on it, I explain that she was the butcher who was going for the brisket. Mark and Bobbie take that as a signal that I've done my job and they can now get me out of there. They twist around, with me in the middle, as if we're a Rockettes line, until we are facing away from the butcher counter. They've managed to propel me a few steps toward the exit when disaster—in the form of a Mazda RX7 pulling up at the loading curb—strikes.

Mark's grip on my arm tightens like a vise. "Too late," he says.

Bobbie's expletive is unprintable. "Maybe there's a back door," she suggests, but Mark is right. It's too late.

I've laid my eyes on Detective Scoones. And while my gut is trying to warn me that my heart shouldn't go there, regions farther south are melting at just the sight of him.

"Walk," Bobbie orders me.

And I try to. Really.

Walk, I tell my feet. *Just put one foot in front of the other.*

I can do this because I know, in my heart of hearts, that if Drew Scoones was still interested in me, he'd have gotten in touch with me after I returned from Boca. And he didn't.

Since he's a detective, Drew doesn't have to wear one of those dark blue Nassau County Police uniforms. Instead, he's got on jeans, a tight-fitting T-shirt and a tweedy sports jacket. If you think that sounds good, you should see him. Chiseled features, cleft chin, brown hair that's naturally a little sandy in the front, a smile that…well, that doesn't matter. He isn't smiling now.

He walks up to me, tucks his sunglasses into his breast pocket and looks me over from head to toe.

"Well, if it isn't Miss Cut and Run," he says. "Aren't you supposed to be somewhere in Florida or something?" He looks at Mark accusingly, as if he was covering for me when he told Drew I was gone.

"Detective Scoones?" one of the uniforms says. "The stiff's in the cooler and the woman who found him is over there." He jerks his head in Fran's direction.

Drew continues to stare at me.

You know how when you were young, your mother always told you to wear clean underwear in case you were in an accident? And how, a little further on, she told you not to go out in hair rollers because you never knew who you might see—or who might see you? And how now your best friend says she wouldn't be caught dead without makeup and suggests you shouldn't, either?

Okay, today, *finally,* in my overalls and Converse sneakers, I get it.

I brush my hair out of my eyes. "Well, I'm back," I say. As if he hasn't known my exact whereabouts. The man is a detective, for heaven's sake. "Been back awhile."

Bobbie has watched the exchange and apparently decided she's given Drew all the time he deserves. "And we've got work to do, so…" she says, grabbing my arm and giving Drew a little two-fingered wave goodbye.

As I back up a foot or two, the store manager sees his chance and places himself in front of Drew, trying to get his attention. Maybe what makes Drew such a good detective is his ability to focus.

Only what he's focusing on is me.

"Phone broken? Carrier pigeon died?" he asks me, taking in Fran, the manager, the meat counter and that Employees Only door, all without taking his eyes off me.

Mark tries to break the spell. "We've got work to do there, you've got work to do here, Scoones," Mark says to him, gesturing toward next door. "So it's back to the alley for us."

Drew's lip twitches. "You working the alley now?" he says.

"If you'd like to follow me," Bill-the-manager, clearly exasperated, says to Drew—who doesn't respond. It's as if waiting for my answer is all he has to do.

So, fine. "You knew I was back," I say.

The man has known my whereabouts every hour of the day for as long as I've known him. And my mother's not the only one who won't buy that he "just happened" to answer this particular call. In fact, I'm willing to bet my children's lunch money that he's taken every call within ten miles of my home since the day I got back.

And now he's gotten lucky.

"*You* could have called *me,*" I say.

"You're the one who said *tomorrow* for our talk and then flew the coop, chickie," he says. "I figured the ball was in your court."

"Detective?" the uniform says. "There's something you ought to see in here."

Drew gives me a look that amounts to *in or out?*

He could be talking about the investigation, or about our relationship.

Bobbie tries to steer me away. Mark's fists are balled. Drew waits me out, knowing I won't be able to resist what might be a murder investigation.

Finally he turns and heads for the cooler.

And, like a puppy dog, I follow.

Bobbie grabs the back of my shirt and pulls me to a halt.

"I'm just going to show him something," I say, yanking away.

"Yeah," Bobbie says, pointedly looking at the buttons on my blouse. The two at breast level have popped. "That's what I'm afraid of."

HARLEQUIN®

Mediterranean
N I G H T S™

Glamour, elegance, mystery and revenge aboard the high seas...

Coming in August 2007...

THE TYCOON'S SON

by
award-winning author
Cindy Kirk

Businessman Theo Catomeris's long-estranged
father is determined to reconnect with his son, so
he hires Trish Melrose to persuade Theo to renew
his contract with Liberty Line. Sailing aboard the
luxurious *Alexandra's Dream* is a rare opportunity for
the single mom to mix business and pleasure. But
an undeniable attraction between Trish and Theo is
distracting her from the task at hand....

HARLEQUIN®

Super Romance®

*Looking for a romantic, emotional
and unforgettable escape?*

*You'll find it this month and every month
with a Harlequin Superromance!*

Rory Gorenzi has a sense of humor and a sense of
honor. She also happens to be good with children.

Seamus Lee, widower and father of four, needs
someone with exactly those traits.

They meet at the Colorado mountain school owned
by Rory's father, where she teaches skiing and
avalanche safety. But Seamus—and his children—
learn more from her than that....

Look for

GOOD WITH CHILDREN
by Margot Early,

*available August 2007, and these other
fantastic titles from Harlequin Superromance.*

REASONS FOR REVENGE

A brand-new provocative miniseries by *USA TODAY*
bestselling author **Maureen Child** begins with

SCORNED
BY THE BOSS

Jefferson Lyon is a man used to having his own way.
He runs his shipping empire from California, and
his admin Caitlyn Monroe runs the rest of his world.
When Caitlin decides she's had enough and needs
new scenery, Jefferson devises a plan to get her back.
Jefferson *never* loses, but little does he know that
he's in a competition....

Don't miss any of the other titles from the
REASONS FOR REVENGE trilogy by
USA TODAY bestselling author **Maureen Child.**

SCORNED BY THE BOSS #1816
Available August 2007

SEDUCED BY THE RICH MAN #1820
Available September 2007

CAPTURED BY THE BILLIONAIRE #1826
Available October 2007

Only from Silhouette Desire!

REQUEST YOUR FREE BOOKS!

2 FREE NOVELS PLUS 2 FREE GIFTS!

Silhouette® Romantic

SUSPENSE

Sparked by Danger, Fueled by Passion!

YES! Please send me 2 FREE Silhouette® Romantic Suspense novels and my 2 FREE gifts. After receiving them, if I don't wish to receive any more books, I can return the shipping statement marked "cancel." If I don't cancel, I will receive 4 brand-new novels every month and be billed just $4.24 per book in the U.S., or $4.99 per book in Canada, plus 25¢ shipping and handling per book plus applicable taxes, if any*. That's a savings of at least 15% off the cover price! I understand that accepting the 2 free books and gifts places me under no obligation to buy anything. I can always return a shipment and cancel at any time. Even if I never buy another book from Silhouette, the two free books and gifts are mine to keep forever.

240 SDN EEX6 340 SDN EEYJ

Name	(PLEASE PRINT)	
Address		Apt. #
City	State/Prov.	Zip/Postal Code

Signature (if under 18, a parent or guardian must sign)

Mail to the Silhouette Reader Service™:
IN U.S.A.: P.O. Box 1867, Buffalo, NY 14240-1867
IN CANADA: P.O. Box 609, Fort Erie, Ontario L2A 5X3

Not valid to current Silhouette Intimate Moments subscribers.

Want to try two free books from another line?
Call 1-800-873-8635 or visit www.morefreebooks.com.

* Terms and prices subject to change without notice. NY residents add applicable sales tax. Canadian residents will be charged applicable provincial taxes and GST. This offer is limited to one order per household. All orders subject to approval. Credit or debit balances in a customer's account(s) may be offset by any other outstanding balance owed by or to the customer. Please allow 4 to 6 weeks for delivery.

Your Privacy: Silhouette is committed to protecting your privacy. Our Privacy Policy is available online at www.eHarlequin.com or upon request from the Reader Service. From time to time we make our lists of customers available to reputable firms who may have a product or service of interest to you. If you would prefer we not share your name and address, please check here. ☐

SRS07

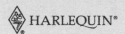
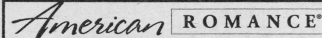

Silhouette®
Romantic
SUSPENSE

COMING NEXT MONTH

#1475 HIGH-STAKES HONEYMOON—RaeAnne Thayne
Olivia Lambert is having one hell of a honeymoon. As if being groomless wasn't bad enough, now she's been kidnapped by a handsome stranger claiming there's a ransom for her life! How is she supposed to trust a man she just met, a man who has threatened her and dragged her across the open ocean—a man who stirs a desire she never felt before?

#1476 SECRET AGENT REUNION—Caridad Piñeiro
Mission: Impassioned
A mysterious betrayal led super spy Danielle Moore to fake her own death. Now she is ready to re-emerge and seek vengeance. But things get complicated when she realizes a mole in her agency is still leaking vital information—and her new partner is the ex-lover she thought dead.

#1477 THE MEDUSA AFFAIR—Cindy Dees
The Medusa Project
When Misty Cordell hears a distress call over her radio, little does she realize a three-hour flight is about to turn into the adventure of a lifetime. "Greg" Harkov has been leading a double life as a spy for too long and discovers Misty could be his key out. But can he trust her with his life… and his heart?

#1478 DANGER AT HER DOOR—Beth Cornelison
A journalist hungry for his big break gets the story of a lifetime when a once-closed rape case resurfaces…and the victim is none other than his reclusive neighbor. But Jack Calhoun wasn't expecting the onslaught of attraction for Megan, or the urge to protect her.

SRSCNM0707